Where the Mistletoe Grows

Shanon Grey

Where The Mistletoe Grows

by Shanon Grey

Copyright, 2022
ISBN: 978-1-957919-02-7
Cover: Jerry Hampton
All Rights Reserved

TOVA PUBLISHING HOUSE
P.O. Box 155
Sharpsburg, GA 30277

Acknowledgments

There are so many I'd like to thank for their continued help and tolerance as I continue to pursue my passion, telling my stories. My family for always encouraging me. My editor for her gentle words. An artist for helping teach me graphic art techniques. And, my readers, for always loving my stories and pushing for more. You lift me up. You make me smile. You brighten my days with your praise. You make me laugh, sharing stories of your own, memories brought on by one of my stories. You have become more than readers. You are my friends. Thank you for that friendship and love.

Dedication

This story is dedicated to all those that have suffered through Covid, be it the virus, vaccinations, or long haul. It is also for those that cared for one another, those that lost loved ones, and those that kept our systems running.

Chapter One

He passed the ornate wood and stone "Welcome to Ruthorford" sign and stopped at the stop sign, looking ahead. In front of him, the narrow, two-lane road opened up, divided by a large park-like median. Plantings, arranged near stones, made a walkway across the end nearest him. Farther down were several benches around a large fountain. Even farther down was a large evergreen, which had probably been a Christmas tree a one time and given a place of honor some years ago. Ruthorford was as pretty as she'd said.

Yes, this would be just fine, he mused as he spotted the large Victorian at the other end of the median. He drove forward, honing in on his destination, ignoring the shops he passed, figuring he'd take a walk later and get his bearings. Right now, he just wanted to lie down, close his eyes, and let oblivion take him. He'd been traveling all day, until the GPS gave out and he'd landed in someone's driveway. When no one answered the door, he drove around until he found a small country store. He was surprised to find they actually had maps, and the owner was more than glad to mark it for him, highlighting his way to the small southern town he hoped would give him the peace of mind to heal.

Leaving his bags in the car, he made his way up the wide stone steps, stopping on the front porch. A rocker moved ever so slightly in the still warm breeze. He found himself smiling. This alone would bring him ease. Opening one of the tall French doors, he walked into the lobby and straight over to the large carved reception counter. No one was there. Hearing voices, he looked to the right to see a woman walk through another set of open French doors with a toddler on her hip.

She smiled at him. "Be right with you," she said and turned back, handing the child to a tall, thin man, grey showing at his temples. "Take her on up, will you? We have company," she kissed the little girl and moved toward the counter.

The other man's smile widened as he watched the women move behind the desk, adoration obvious from his expression. That and desire, he mused. An interesting couple.

"How may I help you?" The woman smiled.

"I'm sorry. I don't have a…a…," he paused for a moment, a crease forming on his forehead, "…reservation," he added, which came out a little more forcefully than intended.

She tilted her head ever so slightly, her silver-blonde hair brushing her shoulders, her blue eyes studying him. "That's okay, we have room for you. I'm Teresa. Welcome to the Abbott Bed & Breakfast." She swung a leather-bound registry around for him to sign and held out a pen. As he took it and their fingers touched, her smile froze, and she quickly released the pen.

"Static," he said simply. "I'm known…for…for it." Blonde hair waved in disarray as he pushed his sunglasses atop his head, keeping the hair from falling across his brow. Brilliant golden eyes, set in a still-tanned face, the hard bone structure softened by the crinkles by his eyes, focused on Teresa.

"Ray Grissom," he said as he put his name and address in the book. He turned it back around and pulled his wallet out of his back jeans pocket.

The front doors swung open and Di and Sim stepped in. "Hey, Teresa! We brought over the order—" Di stopped mid-sentence, her eyes landing on the man who'd turned to look at her. "I'll get the rest," she said, thrusting a basket into Sim's arms, swinging back toward the door, and dashing through it.

Sim shrugged, set the basket on the side table, and retreated through the doors. A sharp whistle stopped Di as she fled down the steps. She turned, watching his fingers fly, *What the hell was that?* he signed.

"I recognize him," she said, crossing the street. All she wanted to do was get away from there.

Sim caught up to her and put his hand on her shoulder, slowing her down. *"From where? When?"* His words settled in her mind softly, like a caress.

"From when I was Diedre Silvermane," she said, walking toward the tea room down Main Street.

Sim followed her inside what was now Di's business after Sassy had bequeathed the tea room to her. He closed and locked the door, turning the "Welcome" sign over. *"Wait. You might recognize him, but he won't recognize you."* His words filled her mind.

She stopped, giving herself time for his words to sink in. Turning, she smiled at him. "Of course, you're right. For a moment, I forgot that I no longer look anything like her." She reached up on tiptoe and kissed him, letting it linger until the heat flowed between them. "Thank you for keeping my head on straight." Smiling, she headed toward the kitchen.

"Oh, no you don't," his tone deeper, a warm caress as the words settled in her mind. *"You can't kiss me like that and just head back to work."* She felt a hint of laughter in her mind.

Even if he was trying to distract her, she appreciated it. She laughed, turned, and ran up a few steps toward their apartment before stopping. *"You're right. There's more where that came from."* She let the thoughts take on a sexy tone as her words filled his mind.

His hand grabbed her hip, and she squealed, running up the stairs, his chuckle settling in her thoughts.

***

Teresa finished the registration and looked at the man in front of her. "Any special requirements?" she asked.

He looked at her for a moment before answering. With a nod, he said, "Patience." He swallowed before continuing. "Maybe a room away from too much noise. I contracted Covid early on. Recovered. Got vaccines. They suspect I might have had a stroke or something somewhere along the line or reacted to the vaccines. I've developed some lingering symptoms, a constant headache, tinnitus, and aphasia. I tend to…to—" he stopped for a moment, frowning, clenched his jaw, and continued, "lose words." When he finished, he wondered why he'd felt compelled to tell her all that. He'd just spent several years running away from it.

"I'm so sorry," she said and connected her hand to his as she handed him the key card she'd already chosen. She let warm energy flow slowly into him. "I've put you on the second floor, all the way back. Your balcony will overlook the creek. It's very peaceful."

Wondering if her choice had been a coincidence, he said, "Thank you," and noticed his headache receding slightly.

"The dining room is open all day. If you prefer, we can deliver food to your room. By the way, that man I handed my daughter to is Mike Yancy. He's our town doctor if you have a need."

"I'm sure I'll be fine. I just need some rest. It's been a long few years. I haven't eaten much today, so I may stop by the dining room in a little while, if that's okay."

"That's fine. We have a full menu, plus daily specials. Today is an Autumn stew. Even though it's warm, Sandra—she's our head chef—hell, she helps run this whole place, had a hankering to get some of our fresh fall veggies into a stew."

"That must be the aroma that's…uh…lur…lur…." When the word wouldn't come, he changed it, "…tempting me." This time he made no apology.

Teresa nodded, "That and the fresh bread they brought from the tea room."

"I will definitely be down later. Thank you so much."

He stepped into the elevator on the other side of a grand staircase and pushed 2, as a voice called out, "Hold that, please."

He held the door open and waited.

"I'll relieve Mike," the sultry voice called back to Teresa as the young woman stepped onto the elevator. "4," she said and glanced at him.

Ray reached over and tapped 4, barely looking at the buttons, his gaze still fixed on her. They said nothing. The air encircled them, enticing. As though compelled, they stared at one another until the elevator stopped on the second floor.

The doors opened, yet he didn't move. All he could think of was the softness of her full lips under his.

As if reading his thoughts, a blush moved up her neck as she glanced at the elevator door still standing open. He stepped off and turned back. As the doors closed, she looked up at him and a faint smile tilted her lips as she whispered, "You have the most amazing eyes." The doors closed and she was gone, her light fragrance lingering with him.

She leaned against the side wall. Never had she felt such yearning, for what she wasn't sure. She swallowed and forced her mind to the toddler waiting for her. As she got off on the fourth floor, she and all of the "descendants" in Ruthorford received a text. <Visitor in the house.>

***

It looked like this place was going to be a good decision, after all. The headache that had become a constant companion was now barely a dull throb. It had eased up enough that he thought he'd take a walk before dinner, get the kinks out of his legs from his long drive. He stepped into the room. A large mahogany sleigh bed dominated the high-ceilinged room. A table and two pub chairs were set in front of the large window. To one side of the window, a French door opened onto a balcony overlooking a long creek and the sweeping back lawn with a large weeping willow to the right. The bath was a definite plus, with a large shower, just what he wanted. Pocketing his key card, he left the room and took the elevator down, looking toward the dining room on his way out. No one was in the lobby, which suited him just fine. Since the illness, he'd found he wasn't much of a conversationalist.

He strode down the steps and crossed the street, turning toward the main part of town. He passed an alleyway, slowing as he got to a bookstore. Chapters. Maybe he'd stop by later and get some reading material. He looked up and saw a sign above another door. The Shoppe of Spells. Intrigued, he walked up the steps and opened the door. The scent of lavender filled the air.

"Be right with you," a man's voice called out from behind a door.

He looked around. Not at all what he expected from the façade. It appeared to be more of a gift shop with well-lit shelves and bottles.

"Disappointed?" a man asked as he stepped out from the door, closing it behind him.

"A little," he laughed.

"Trust me, there was a time," the man said. "I'm Dorian. Welcome to The Shoppe of Spells—gift shop and apothecary."

"Apothecary?"

"Local pharmacy."

"Ahhh. Do you fill prescriptions?"

"I do. What can I do for you?"

"I have this prescription I haven't filled but promised I would, just in case."

Dorian took the script and looked at it. "Amitriptyline. Have you ever used this before?"

"No. I have these…headaches—"

A screen door slammed in the back. "I just got the most incredible pumpkins—" She stopped when she saw the man standing at the counter in the front. "I'm sorry." She set the small pumpkins down on a table in the kitchen and moved into the front room, casually wiping her hands on her jeans before holding one out, "I'm Morgan."

Ray looked at the beautiful woman with magnificent green eyes and glossy red curls and took her hand. "Ray Grissom," he said. "I'm staying at the bed and breakfast."

As he took her hand, she blinked and looked at him, quickly lowering her gaze. She let go and turned to Dorian. "I'm sorry. I didn't mean to interrupt. I was going to prep these pumpkins and take them to the sisters for pies." Her gaze went from Dorian to the paper in his hand, giving an almost imperceptible frown.

"Well, I've got things here, so you go prep," he said and gave her a slight nod.

She took a deep breath and turned. "Nice meeting you, Ray. Enjoy your stay."

"Nice meeting you, too." He turned back to Dorian.

"I don't keep this in stock," Dorian said, holding onto the script. "I'll have to order it."

"Oh, that's okay. I haven't needed it, so far. It's just in case the…the…headaches get worse."

"Ray, I'm going to be honest. This is a drug with some potentially serious side effects. We have an excellent doctor in town, Mike Yancy, who might be able to give you something as effective but with fewer risks."

Ray laughed. "That's the second mention of your doctor since I got here. He must be something. I'll think about it. Why don't you hold onto that script for now."

"Will do. Let me know if you need something. We carry over-the-counter remedies that work pretty well, too."

"Thanks. I'll remember that."

He hadn't closed the door before Morgan walked into the room. "He needs to see Mike, Dorian. I don't like what I saw."

"What did you see?"

"You know I'm not perfect. But I saw a vagueness around his head. The aura was dullish on one side, not vibrant, like the other."

"I'm calling Teresa," Dorian said.

Unaware of the conversation transpiring behind him, Ray pulled out his phone when it pinged and read the text.

<Are you there? What do you think?>

<I'm here, walking down the street.> He looked up. <near Sassy's Tea Room. Thanks. I know this will help.>

<Try the brioche French toast. It's amazing. And Sim's French onion soup. Gotta run. Now I'm hungry.>

He laughed and slipped the phone back into his pocket.

"Yoo-hoo! Hi. Over here."

He stopped and looked across the median. An older woman stood on a porch waving at him. He waved back. She waved again, motioning him over. He crossed the median, stopping at the gate of the fence surrounding the house.

"You are just the person I need," she said. "Come on. I have some pies ready for the Bed & Breakfast."

"Me?"

"You don't see anyone else, do you?" She disappeared into the house. He went up the steps but hesitated following her.

"Go on. She won't bite." Another woman sat on a swing, shelling peas. "Besides, she's had her shots." She laughed at her own joke.

Ray pulled open the screen door, its squeak bringing a sudden memory of a childhood long gone.

"Back here."

He followed the voice and the aroma of spices down a long hallway into a kitchen.

"I'm Miss Grace, and that worthless woman still sitting on the porch is my sister, Alice. I'm so glad you stopped by. None of the boys have happened by, and these are still warm." She pointed to two large bags filled with boxes. "You're Ray. I called Teresa and she said you might be down this way."

He just nodded, knowing he wouldn't get a word in edgewise.

"Thank you. Tell them you get an extra-large piece." With that she shooed him back outside, his arms carrying the bags. "Don't dawdle."

He nodded again and let her open the gate for him. So much for a casual walk before dinner. He hurried down the sidewalk.

The women he'd share an elevator with stepped out of a shop and looked at him. "Need help with that?"

"I think I've…got it."

"Don't be silly. Give me one of those," she insisted and took a bag from him, walking toward the Bed & Breakfast with him.

"I'm Ray. We didn't get to exchange names earlier in the elevator."

She looked at him. "Oh, that would be my sister, Bonnie. She went over earlier to babysit. I'm Claire."

"Oh. You look very much alike."

"We should. We're twins."

"Fraternal?"

She stopped and looked at him. "No. Identical. You don't think we look alike."

"Not identical. Her voice is deeper and she seems shyer. And her eyes are…different. Plus, the hair." He didn't mention that, now that he stood next to her, she was nothing like the woman who'd invaded his very being.

Claire started walking again. "Interesting," she said mostly to herself.

Teresa held the door open for them. "Ray, I am so sorry. I was going to send Dorian, but he had something to do and said you'd just left."

"Glad I could…be of ser…help. I think I'm about ready for dinner now. Where should I put these? He retrieved the bag from Claire and followed Teresa through the dining room and into the kitchen. "I'll have whatever smells so good," he said, setting the bags where Teresa pointed.

"Go have a seat. I'll have it out shortly. Thanks, again."

"Let me go get my luggage and I'll…be right in."

Chapter Two

Claire stepped off the elevator and followed the dulcet tones of her sister's voice to the baby's bedroom. She stopped in the doorway and listened to her sister, leaning over the crib, crooning softly. That was another way they were different. Her sister had one of the most amazing voices she'd ever heard. Hers was good, but not like Bonnie's.

Bonnie looked up and smiled, putting her finger to her lips. In response, Claire nodded toward the library and headed that way. She'd no more than grabbed a soda from the mini fridge when Bonnie stepped in. "I'll take one."

Claire handed her sister a drink and sat on the couch. "I think you have an admirer," she teased, taking a swig.

Bonnie looked at her, popping the top. "Who?"

"That guy named Ray."

Bonnie's brows came together in a frown.

"Oh. That's right. You don't know his name. He now knows yours because I told him."

When Bonnie still didn't react, she added, "Guy in the elevator."

"Oh," Bonnie said and sat up straighter.

"I was coming over and saw this guy toting bags for the sisters and offered to help. He introduced himself, thinking I was you."

"Oh." Bonnie's voice was barely above a whisper. Claire tended to get all the attention because she had all the personality.

"As soon as I corrected him, he said, now that I'd talked, he knew we were different."

"Really?"

"Yep. Voice. Shyness. Eyes. He doesn't even think we look that much alike. He's down there having dinner right now if you want to go down."

"I'm busy."

"No, you're not. I'm here. Go down."

"I can't."

"We brought pies. Go get us some pie."

"I am kinda hungry."

Claire just smiled and sipped her drink, watching her *little* sister, by a mere two minutes, head to the elevator.

Bonnie almost lost her nerve, hesitating in the doorway to the dining room. But, at that moment, Teresa looked up from where she was talking to Ray at a table in the back. "Just the person," she said, motioning her over.

Forcing a smile, Bonnie walked over. "I just came down to get some pie."

"I was just telling Ray about Fashion Flare. He wants to get a present for the woman who recommended Ruthorford to him."

Her heart sank. A girlfriend. Of course, he'd have a girlfriend, a guy that good looking. She took a deep breath. "I'd be happy to help any way I can."

"You remember Gillian Raine, don't you?" Teresa asked.

Bonnie thought back. The name rang a bell. "Sounds familiar."

"The writers' group that comes in the spring. He just did her latest cover."

"Oh! Gillian. I love her books." She really did. And she also loved the fact that Gillian was in her sixties. You're an artist. We have a fantastic gallery here, next to our shop."

"Hi. I'm Ray, by the way. We sort of ran into each other earlier. I also…met your sister. She helped me after the sisters corralled me into carrying pies. I hear that's a com…com…regular practice around here."

"It sure is. Everyone's fair game." She laughed, unthinkingly pushing her hair back from her face. "I'm Bonnie, by the way." When his eyes met hers, her shyness kicked in, and her eyes dropped.

He loved the way her eyes lit up when she smiled. And the faint tint of pink that flushed her cheeks when he spoke to her.

Sandra arrived carrying a try. Teresa stepped back and let Sandra serve Ray's dinner.

He looked at Bonnie. "Join me?"

She blushed harder. "I can't. I'm busy," she added and glanced at Teresa before saying, "Stop by the store any time and we'll be glad to help you find something for Gillian. I know for a fact that she loves our scarves."

"I will," he said. "Another time, maybe."

She nodded and followed Sandra back to the kitchen.

Sandra no sooner had let the door close behind them than she turned on Bonnie. "Seriously? That hottie invited you to sit down and share a meal, and you said no."

"I know. But I'm babysitting."

"With all of us here, I think we can spare you."

"He does have the cutest mouth. I love the way his lip quirks up on one side."

Teresa walked into the kitchen. She looked at Bonnie, concentrating on what Bonnie had just said, thinking. "It does...doesn't it?" She pulled out her phone and hit a number. "Mike, I need you to come here. Everything's okay with the family. I'm concerned about one of the guests."

A crash sounded from the dining room. When Teresa pushed through the door, Ray was sitting at the table, staring at his hand. The water glass was on the floor.

She hit *one* again. "Mike, ambulance," she said into the phone and rushed toward the table, Bonnie and Sandra behind her. Ray looked up, a frown forming. He tried to say something and couldn't. One side of his mouth wasn't moving.

Bonnie stepped around Teresa and put her hand on his shoulder. "It's okay. Just relax. Mike is on his way." She watched as calm eased his expression.

He tried to nod but wasn't sure if he had.

Sandra removed the food from the table, pulling the table back. Bonnie kept her hand on his shoulder, speaking softly.

Teresa heard Mike run in and spoke. "I think he's stroking."

Mike nodded and they all moved back as he began working. The gurney arrived, and the EMTs placed Ray on it.

"Call Sim and Morgan. They are quicker than the machines. I need to know what I'm dealing with. Bonnie, ride with us."

Bonnie nodded and followed them out. As she watched them load Ray into the back of the ambulance, she pulled a scrunchy from her pocket and pulled her hair back, harnessing the thick sable mass into a ponytail. She stepped into the back of the ambulance, where Mike made room for her beside the gurney. She sat on the bench and placed her hand on Ray's arm. "Ray, I want you to concentrate on my voice. In it, you will feel a rhythm. We are going to slow your heartbeat and pulse with that rhythm. Can you blink to let me know you understand?"

He blinked.

She looked at Mike. He nodded and she proceeded to do what they had practiced over and over, using her talent to ease a patient's fear and steady the heartbeat and pulse. Mostly, she used it on the young descendants who got injured. She'd only done it twice on adults, once on Sandra's sister and once on Mike. Both had claimed it had worked well.

However, Ray was an outsider. Once this was over, he probably wouldn't want to be around her again. She knew, having watched descendants in the real world, how outsiders reacted to their different and unique abilities. Right now, she didn't care. Ray was in danger and she had the ability to help him, so she would.

She felt his pulse spike and pushed calm into him. "Listen to my voice. Feel the rhythm. Let's match our rhythms. She took a deep breath and sought the rhythm, gradually slowing it.

His eyes remained on hers, as if she anchored him. She gave his shoulder a gentle squeeze.

***

By the time she unlocked the door to her apartment over the shop, she couldn't think of anything but sleep. Her sister's voice made her jump.

"What are you doing here?"

"Worrying about you. How's Ray?"

She walked over and slumped down on the couch next to her sister. "I think he'll be okay. I don't know all the things that they did, but I've never seen so many people work in concert so fast. Sim, Morgan, Mike—even me." She leaned her head over on her sister's shoulder. "I was so scared for him."

Claire handed her the can of Coke. "It's still cold."

"Thanks," Bonnie said and took a deep drink. "He had a clot either in or going to his brain. I don't understand much, but Mike said that Ray had told Teresa he'd had one before, or maybe it was the same one and had gotten thicker." She shrugged. "Anyway, they gave him something. Then, ended up taking him to surgery. I went with all of them but stood in the corner, wondering just why I was there."

"Not fond of blood, huh?"

She pushed into her sister. "You know we don't do blood."

"Yeah, but you have that incredible talent. You should be a nurse."

Bonnie sat up and looked at her sister, who had a twinkle in her eyes. "Eww. No way." She pushed herself up from the couch. "I'm going to bed. I'm supposed to work in the kitchen tomorrow. Are you staying here tonight?"

"Oh. Sandra said for you not to come in. Get some sleep. I'm headed back to the house. I don't want to leave mom all night."

Bonnie turned around. "Want me to come with you?"

"Good heavens, no." She leaned over and kissed her sister on the cheek. "I can feel your exhaustion. Call me tomorrow. I'll lock the door when I leave. Go to bed."

Bonnie nodded and headed down the hall to her bedroom.

***

Mike slipped into bed next to his warm, soft wife, grateful every moment he had her.

"How is he?"

"I think he'll be okay. Ended up using a retrievable stent to remove a clot. I'm still not sure if what happened today was a continuation from before or a new problem. We had to work fast. I can't tell you how grateful I am to have descendants to work with."

"I feel that way every day—about you, outsider," she said and snuggled into him. "Is he going to be all right?"

"I know that having you call and tell me what you felt when he signed in gave me a lot of information to work with, saving a lot of time. However, it's the brain. Dr. Albert came, thank heavens. I still don't know for sure what to expect. Whatever it was, I feel certain he's going to need some rehab."

"He can stay here as long as he needs. We'll move him down to the first floor."

"Have I told you how wonderful you are?"

"Not in the last ten minutes."

He chuckled and nuzzled into her neck, inhaling her scent. "I have to keep my phone on. Sorry."

"No. It's okay. Get some sleep. He's in good hands."

***

When Teresa saw Mike cross the lobby, she smiled. For someone going on less than five hours of sleep, he sure looked rested. The love in her heart must have shown in her eyes because his smile spread until his eyes twinkled.

"There are my girls," he said and kissed Teresa and turned to Aby, who held up her chubby arms.

"Watch out, she's been finger-fooding the melon."

He chuckled. "Best way to eat it," he said and kissed her sticky fingers. "Yum," he said, pretending to take a bite of a finger, sending Aby into fits of laughter. She then pulled his hand to her mouth and slobbered all over his fingers.

As he wiped his hands on the napkin and took his seat at the table, Sandra was right there with a pot of coffee.

"I'll just take some fruit—"

She interrupted, "Oh, no, you won't. I have an omelet with your name on it, already coming up." Without waiting, she turned and headed to the kitchen.

"Maybe you apprenticed her too well," he said to Teresa and took a deep drink of coffee. "Oh, this is good."

The kitchen door had barely swung closed when Sandra backed through, carrying two plates. She set them in front of Teresa and Mike. Cheese omelets and bacon with small fruit cups on the plate. "There. That should get both of you going. You at the clinic and Teresa with the holiday planning meeting."

Mike looked at his plate. It did look good. "Ah, yes, it's that time of year. Pumpkins and pumpkin pie will soon be everywhere."

"I liked the idea that we dedicated Halloween décor to strictly October and Halloween this year. That will make more of an impact for the Thanksgiving theme."

He wasn't listening but looking at his phone. "Uh-huh," he said absently.

"And we going to dig up the graveyard and set bones all around," she said and waited.

"Wait. What?"

"Now that I have your attention...." Teresa said, laughing.

Chapter Three

"How's Luke?" Di's voice carried from the lobby as she walked toward the dining room. She stepped over to the sideboard, grabbed a mug, added coffee, and carried it over to the table, setting it next to Mike before planting a kiss, first on Teresa's cheek, then on top of Aby's head, and finally on Mike's cheek.

"Good morning, daughter," Mike said, grinning at Di. No matter how they'd acquired her, he loved her as if she were his own.

"Good morning, Dad. Mom. Aby."

Aby squealed.

Teresa studied Di. "Luke?"

Di frowned. "The man at the counter yesterday."

"Oh. That's Ray Grissom. I figured there was more to that exit yesterday than what you said. Just how do you know that man? Different name, but you recognized him from somewhere."

"Luke Grissom is an artist. I knew him in my Silvermane days. When I saw him, I forgot that I don't look like her anymore and panicked. Sim set me straight."

"And where is Sim this morning."

"Setting up for a brunch. He woke me this morning to fill me in about the surgery."

Teresa raised her brow.

"Okay, he sent mind messages all night long, until I told him to stop. Sometimes he forgets that I get images and not just words. That surgery was...uh...how do I say this...."

"Incredible? Life-saving?" Mike supplied.

"Bloody. Kinda oogie," Di said with a laugh. "How's the patient doing?"

"He had a good night," Mike supplied. "I'll know more when I get there." He stood. "Speaking of which, I'm going to run. I want to be there when he regains consciousness." He kissed everyone, grabbed his bag from behind the lobby's counter, and was out the door in a hurry.

"Does he ever slow down?" Di asked.

"Not often. He was exhausted when he got to bed. But, he was better this morning."

"I'm sure your energy push had something to do with that."

"Maybe. Tell me more about this man. He said this place was recommended by one of our writers. He does book covers for her."

Di's fork stopped halfway to her mouth. "What? That doesn't make sense. He's such a remarkable artist. Book covers?"

Teresa nodded. "Maybe that's why the different names."

"Authors use pen names. Why not artists?" Di studied her mother for a moment. "Wait. I know you know more than you're saying. What did you see?"

Taking a sip of coffee and putting a handful of dry cereal in front of Aby, Teresa turned to Di. "He's had a rough few years. He contracted Covid early on, when it was at its worst. They didn't have to intubate him, but he was in the hospital for over a month. He was one sick guy. Afterward, he got the vaccines, then a booster. At some point, he started having constant headaches. At the same time, tinnitus started. Then a weakness in his left hand and aphasia. They said he might have had a mild stroke, but I didn't get an impression of any aggressive treatment. Given what the medical community has been through, he might be lucky he got treatment at all."

Sadness showed in Di's eyes. "Oh, my lord. I can't imagine what he's been through."

Teresa tilted her head. "You can't?"

Di smiled. "Look. I had amnesia. It was my art that helped me pull out of it. I always had my art. The artist I knew him to be was left-handed." She looked down at her hands. "I can't imagine not being able to draw." She drank some coffee, looking out the window. Turning back to Teresa, she spoke softly, "So, did he have another stroke or more of the first?"

"I don't know. But I know Mike and his team will do whatever is necessary to save him and as much of his brain as possible. He did mention rehab last night."

"Do you think there's anything I can do to help?"

"He didn't seem to recognize you, but your voice is the same. Let's play it by ear." She reached out and put her hand over Di's. "I don't want you put in jeopardy."

"Mom, what you and Mike, Jenn, and all of Ruthorford, did for me is beyond anything I could have imagined. I feel pretty secure. All my records are changed. Those women I was are no more. I just had a momentary setback. Fear. I'm not afraid anymore. I want to help."

"We'll see. I know you're a certified art therapist and have helped some children at the hospital." She thought for a moment. "Maybe through Kat. Her fame as KC might be used to camouflage yours. I know you aren't Silvermane anymore. And, to the world, she is dead. But…." She shook her head. "First, let's see how Ray's doing and what Mike thinks."

"I heard Bonnie really stepped up, too," Di commented as she nodded in agreement.

"She did. I am so proud of her. I guess being around here—cooking and being around people more has helped. For a while I was worried. She was becoming more and more withdrawn. Even as a child she was introverted, but later…," Teresa stopped, thinking, then smiled. "I'm so glad she decided to share her culinary talent with us. What a better, more appreciative crowd to boost your confidence than Ruthorford?"

"It amazes me how different Bonnie and Claire are for identical twins."

"Not so much when you remember they are descendants. Think about Dorian and Eryk."

"True. You sure the guys aren't fraternal? I mean, with the eye color and those differences in abilities."

Teresa just laughed. "When was the last time you were in their presence together?"

"The other night." She thought about it and laughed. "You're right, of course. Not being a descendant, I tend to forget. Yet, with Bonnie being so introverted—"

"Good morning." Bonnie walked into the room.

"Speak of the devil," Teresa said. "What are you doing up so early?"

"I couldn't sleep anymore. Any word on Ray?" Bonnie asked and got some coffee before sitting next to Teresa.

"Mike just left. I'm sure he'll let us know. Did you get a read on him before you left?"

Bonnie shook her head. "Once he went under, it was like a disconnect. I don't know if I could have influenced his heart rate or not at that point. After he was taken to recovery, I momentarily put my hand on his arm but was afraid to try anything. I didn't want to risk waking him."

"I know Mike is so happy you helped. You are really coming into your own, sweetie." Teresa patted her hand, taking on Bonnie's memories of the days before. She had to fight a smile when the image of the elevator passed through her mind. *"Well, I'll be. Looks like she really is coming into herself,"* she mused to herself.

"Di, if you don't mind watching your sister, I'm going to go call Gillian. I want her to know about Ray."

"No problem. Sim won't need me for a few hours."

"I thought I'd see if I could help Sandra with the breakfast crowd. I know people will be in, wanting to hear the latest."

"Thanks," Teresa said. "You're probably right, given our town." She shook her head as she walked toward the lobby, just as Jasmine and Eryk walked through the door. "Grab a seat. Di will catch you up and Bonnie will feed you."

"What?" Jasmine asked, looking confused.

"Don't even try," Di called from the dining room. "She knows Morgan called you as soon as she could."

"Can't keep a secret around here for nothin'," Jasmine quipped. "Geesh."

Teresa's laughter carried as the elevator doors closed.

***

Mike stood at the foot of the bed, studying the patient. Sometimes observation from afar did more than close up. The patient had his eyes closed but wasn't asleep.

Ray's eyes fluttered open and he was focused on Mike. "I suppose I owe you for my life." His voice came our strong and clear.

"It was a team effort," Mike said. "You sound good. How are you feeling?"

"I've been lying here taking a self-assessment." He lifted his left arm. "Yesterday, in the dining room, my fingers started to tingle, and I couldn't grasp the glass or the spoon. Then, things got fuzzy. Now, no tingling at all. He put his finger to his thumb. Feels fine."

"Your voice sounds good. And no stuttering."

"I still have a headache, and the tinnitus is still there. Not as severe. Thank you."

The door opened and a woman walked in, "Good morning, Mike. Ray."

Mike smiled. "Good morning, Dr. Albert. Ray, this is the brilliant neurosurgeon that performed the procedure on you last night on very short notice."

"Ray and I met earlier, didn't we?"

"I am so grateful. Yet, so confused. Apparently, the doctors that treated me earlier missed something."

Dr. Albert looked at Mike before speaking. "I can't speak for what happened before, but the records I looked at didn't mention any treatment."

"But they said…." Ray's voice trailed off.

Dr. Albert walked over, put her hand on his wrist, and looked at the monitor. His pulse and blood pressure were rising.

There was a knock on the door and it opened. "Oh, I'm sorry, I didn't know you had company." Bonnie started to step back.

"Wait," Mike said.

"Yes, sir?"

"Steady him, please."

Dr. Albert frowned at them. Ignoring her, Bonnie walked over, dropped what she was carrying on the chair, and, giving a tentative smile to Ray, placed her hand on his shoulder. His pulse immediately steadied and started to slow.

Dr. Albert kept her hand on his wrist as she watched the monitor. She took a deep breath right before Mike took her arm and pulled her hand from Ray's wrist. "You will inadvertently have your pulse slowed, which you might not want to do right now," he said, chuckling.

She nodded, smiled, and stepped to the end of the bed.

Ray turned his head and gave Bonnie a slight grin. The quirky little lift to one side of his mouth was gone, making Bonnie realize it had been a symptom, not a feature. She gave his shoulder a slight squeeze.

Mike spoke softly. "Now would be a good time to tell him what you have learned," he said to Dr. Albert.

"Oh. Right," she said. She watched the interplay between the girl, her patient, and the monitor. When she'd agreed to join the clinic and the Abbott House Foundation, she'd learned things she'd never known existed. Thus far, she'd never really had a chance to see it in action. The fact that Ray was an "outsider," as Mike had said, left her with too many questions. She'd table them for later with Mike.

"Ray, we know so little about Covid. It hit fast and mutated over and over, thankfully becoming less deadly as it did so. You were hit with the first strain, the deadliest. Having survived that, you were vaccinated. I have read about cases of long Covid that produced strokes. I think that's what your doctors thought. I have also read of people reacting to the vaccines and boosters similarly to what you have shown. I think your doctors acted in good faith. They treated the symptoms, not finding anything else. Trust me, since yesterday, you were scanned and examined as many ways as possible," she stopped to take a breath and left out mentioning the scans performed by Sim and Morgan. "We found a small clot and used a retrievable stent to remove it. I think, and I'm still speculating here, that this was the only clot you've had. The prognosis for a full recovery from this is excellent. However, as to the symptoms you were experiencing before this event, I can't speak. If you are willing to do your rehab here, we can do more studies and watch you. If you want to return to Virginia, I can forward your records."

Ray didn't even have to think about it. "I came here on a fluke to rest, recover, and get better. It apparently saved my life. I would like to stay. I don't know what's involved in the rehab, but I'll find a place—"

"You have a place," Mike interrupted. "With us, for as long as you want."

He looked at Mike. "Are you sure? I don't know how long it will be."

"Well, you met my wife. When she says something is so, it is. We all agree. You are welcome here."

Ray couldn't help it, he turned to Bonnie, who nodded. "Well, I guess it's settled. When do we start?"

"Well, we had to put a hole in your femoral artery, and you will be on some blood thinners, so you will rest here for a day or so and then move to the Bed & Breakfast on restricted activity for a bit while we evaluate your progress."

"Okay," he agreed, then looked around. "How about food? Can I have some food?"

Bonnie chuckled and removed her hand. "I think he's stable enough."

"It won't be steak, but the menu comes from the B & B, so I think you'll be happy," Mike said as he pulled out his phone, texting. "Bonnie, I'm going to send you to the cafeteria to pick it up. Then, if you can, sit with him while he eats. We'll raise the head while you eat, but then I want you as flat as you can stand for today. If you have problems with the spoon, don't fight it, let Bonnie help. She's an amazing assistant. I know. She helped me after I was injured in a tornado."

Bonnie blushed as she moved out of the room. "I'll be back in a minute," she said quietly, her beautiful voice flowing over them like silk.

Ray's eyes widened. "Oh, crap. I forgot. I was supposed to call Gillian last night about the cover for her novel."

"Teresa said to tell you she was going to call her. I want you to concentrate on feeling better. No stress. Got it?"

Chapter Four

Mike stopped the car at the edge of town so Ray could take in the view.

"Damn. I was here just a few days ago, and it now looks totally different."

"Never underestimate the power of a town run by women."

Ray looked at the median. It had been transformed into a sea of orange, purple, and yellow chrysanthemums. Pumpkins surrounded the fountain and each bench was anchored by more fall florals. The evergreen was decked out in fall colors, as were the houses and the shops along the way with wreaths and planters galore. The lampposts had fall-colored garlands twining their way up to the lights.

Mike drove slowly so Ray could take it all in, since there was no way he would be walking it any time soon.

"I've never seen a Christmas tree decorated for fall," he said, the excitement in his voice.

"If you behave," Mike teased, "you can sit on the porch and look down Main Street. Wait until you see it at night." Mike pulled up in front of the B & B. It, too, had been decked out for Fall, with pots of flowers and pumpkins lining the wide steps and garlands of amber and orange draped in swags along the porch rails. Each window had an orange and purple wreath, and swags hung down under the lights on either side of the French doors.

"Stay," Mike commanded, got out, and came around the SUV, opening Ray's door.

"I can't do anything?"

"Not for a day, so I can see how you're doing. It's against Dr. Albert's better judgment that I broke you out early as it is. So, take my arm and go one step at a time, stopping on each step, or you'll go right back into the hospital."

"And, as to the decorations, I'm warning you. You haven't seen anything yet."

Ray obeyed him, taking it slow, moving one foot at a time, stopping on each step. By the time they'd reached the porch, Teresa was holding the door open, a beautiful smile on her lips.

"Welcome home, Ray. I took the liberty of changing your room. You'll be on the first floor, down in the back, where it's quiet, but no steps to climb. I am so glad you are okay. We're here to help you get better. Believe that."

"Thank you," he said, a slight blush dusting his cheeks. "I hate putting you all out."

"This town is one large family. You will meet all of them eventually, I'm sure. Oh, and the sisters have already sent you a get-well pie, all for you. And you didn't even have to carry it."

He laughed as she took his arm and led him inside. He felt warmth pass up his arm until it flooded his body, and he suddenly felt better than he had since he'd been taken down by Covid.

"Not too much," Mike said casually, knowing what Teresa was doing. Then, looking at Ray as if he was addressing him, he said. "Take it slow."

Teresa looked at Mike and smiled innocently. "He will. I promise."

Mike just shook his head and looked toward the ceiling.

"Damn," Ray exclaimed as he stepped into the lobby. "Sorry, ma'am," he said as he looked around inside the Bed & Breakfast. It had been transformed into an autumn wonderland. "This is gorgeous." It sparkled and twinkled and shone in festive autumn colors. "Who did this?"

"What?" Teresa asked. "Oh. We did."

"Who's we? You have a decorating company?"

"No, the town. Wait until you see us change it from Fall to Winter overnight. Well, almost overnight. The day after Thanksgiving, the whole town comes together, Fall is taken down, and Winter goes up. I hope you'll plan to stay with us until Christmas. We do love our holidays."

"Let's get him to his room. I want to examine him and make sure we haven't done any damage bringing him here." He took Ray's arm and let Teresa lead them down the hallway. She opened the door to a Victorian room, done in autumn colors but more muted. A large four-poster stood next to the door to the bath. He could see handrails in the bath.

"This room is accessible," Teresa said, adding, "I need to get back. I'll have dinner brought to you here tonight. We'll see how you feel tomorrow. Can I get you anything in the meantime?"

"Bonnie," he said and flushed when Teresa smiled, rushing on, "I didn't mean it that way. I mean is she around?"

"She's helping out in the kitchen. We're feeding the town tonight because of all the decorating. It's an excuse to get everyone together, but we want them to know how grateful we are. Oh, and the noise might carry a bit. I'm sorry. We can be a bit rowdy. I'll see if Bonnie can stop by later."

"If she wants to, that is," he said. "I haven't seen her since she helped me out that day after surgery."

"I'll let her know you asked after her. How's that?"

"That would be fine. Thank you."

She walked to the door and turned back around. "Oh, I put your phone on the charger and your laptop next to it by the bed. There's a lapboard on the bed. In the closet, there's a bed desk. Mike can get it, if you prefer."

"I'm fine. You've gone to so much trouble already. Thank you."

She smiled and pulled the door closed behind her.

Ray watched her leave before turning to Mike. "Why do I feel like I'm a ten-year-old around her?"

Mike just laughed and helped him off with his jacket. "It's a gift she has. Hell, I feel that way sometimes."

***

"Bonnie, if he didn't want to see you, he wouldn't have asked," Teresa said and watched Bonnie wipe the counter harder.

"He was just being nice, I'm sure."

"Poppycock," Teresa said and walked over and laid her hand over the one with the sponge. "Slow down. It's clean. Tell me what's going on." She could feel her withdrawing, pulling away. Most of the time, Bonnie stayed in the kitchen, away from the crowds. Even though she knew everyone out there, she became almost paralyzed with panic when she had to confront all of them together, so Teresa let her stay in the kitchen, cooking, serving up plates, and cleaning. For someone with the gift to calm others, she could do little to calm herself.

"He knows what I can do. He looked at me while I was helping him eat and I saw that look."

"What look?"

"The one where they think I'm a freak."

"In case you haven't noticed, sweetpea, we are all freaks."

Bonnie spun on her. "He's an outsider!" she almost shouted.

"And…." Teresa just looked at her, waiting.

"…and, I really like him." Her voice came out in almost a whisper. "I don't want him to laugh at me."

Teresa stepped over and pulled her into her arms. "Oh, Bonnie, no one thinks you're a freak, and no one is going to laugh at you. Least of all, Ray. Trust me, I know these things." With that, she gave her own little push.

Bonnie stepped back and rubbed her arms, smiling, just as Mike walked in.

"Hey, ladies. Mind if I join?"

"Not at all," Teresa said and moved into his arms, giving a push of energy.

"Thanks. I needed that," he said and looked at Bonnie. "Bonnie, I need your help."

Teresa saw the trepidation on the girl's face.

So did Mike. "It's not like I'm going to ask you to jump off the roof and fly," he said and felt Teresa's elbow in his rib. "I need you to help me with Ray."

"I don't know," Bonnie began and grabbed the sponge again, making large circles on the counter.

Not knowing what she'd just confessed to Teresa, Mike blundered on, "It's not like I can let him walk around with a blood pressure cuff. But he knows you can help him control it, and that way, he can start to do more. I already asked him if I could ask you—" He jumped sideways. "Ow! Damn, woman, would you stop poking me?"

Teresa made a face at him.

Resigned, Bonnie looked at Teresa. "It's all right, Teresa. It's a guy thing. The denseness, I mean," Bonnie said, and planting her hands on her hips, she gave Mike a look of disdain.

Teresa swung around and looked at her. "Well, damn. I wondered when that woman would show up."

Mike looked from Teresa to Bonnie, confused. "What am I missing?" Mike asked. "I just want some help for Ray."

Bonnie smiled at Teresa. "You're right. I need to get over my insecurities. Plus, Mike needs my talent. That comes first. I'll deal with it—somehow."

"I'm here for you. But, first, I'm going to take him his dinner and smooth the way, probably better than the doctor—the outsider doctor—did." With that, Teresa fixed a tray and backed through the door, followed by Mike.

"What did I do?" His voice grew faint as the door closed. Bonnie leaned against the counter and put the sponge down, her fingers trembling. *Why can't I be more like Claire?"*

***

Ray stood in front of the bathroom mirror, looking at his reflection. He squinted and leaned forward. He smiled. More like pulled his lips across his teeth, tight. At least it looked equilateral. How had he not noticed? He'd definitely noticed the fatigue, as well as the tremor and weakness in his hand.

He held out his hand. Steady. He held out the other, just in case, next to the left. Both were as steady as they'd once been. He made fists. Not at tight as he'd like, but they performed better than he remembered.

A knock drew his attention. "Coming," he said, stepping into the room. He took the doorknob and pulled open the door.

Teresa's card was in the lock. "Sorry. I thought you were in bed. Mike told me to bring you something."

He stepped back. "No problem. I probably should have been. But, after 2 days, I'm about bedded out."

She chuckled. "Well, it's just as well. It's better to eat this sitting up." She walked past him to the table in front of the window, set up like his previous room.

"Smells heavenly," he said, as the aroma teased his nose as she passed.

"Ham, bean, and corn soup with corn logs.

She saw his frown. "Cornbread baked in long shapes." She set the tray to one side, set his place setting, put the plate down, and set the bowl on it. "I brought sweet tea. I hope that's all right."

He pulled out the chair and sat down. "You really don't have to go to all this trouble." He put the napkin in his lap and picked up the spoon, studying it.

"Oh…I didn't think…can you…?"

He tightened his fingers around the spoon, showing her. "I'm good."

"I am so glad. Mike said you should rest. Leave this on the table. I'll send Bonnie in later to pick it up."

He stopped with the spoon not yet in his mouth. "Only if she wants to." He put the spoonful of soup in his mouth and made a sound. "Wow. This is so good."

"It is, isn't it. Just what the doctor ordered." She studied him for a moment. "Ray, I'm going to be honest with you. Bonnie is not like her sister. She's extremely shy."

He took another bite and stopped, looking at her, thinking back to the woman who had helped steady him. He smiled. "I know she's quieter. But shy? She's amazing."

"And the fact that you know about her talent worries her."

"It shouldn't. She helped save my life. Plus, she has this voice…." He let his words die.

"You should hear her sing, which she doesn't do nearly enough. She croons to Aby when she sits with her. Aby has gotten to where she asks for *Bommie* whenever I try to sing."

He laughed. "Oh, sorry."

"No worries. I know I can't hold a candle to that voice."

"Well, please ask her to stop by. I really do want to thank her. Maybe I can talk to her some and not just while she's keeping my pulse steady."

Teresa laughed, her eyes twinkling.

"I don't think that came out like I meant."

She patted him on the shoulder. "You are definitely better. When you are done, please get in bed. I don't want Mike hauling your butt back to the clinic tonight."

"Yes, ma'am."

By the time Bonnie knocked lightly on the door, he'd finished eating, brushed his teeth, and sent a text to Gillian.

"Come on in."

Bonnie stepped into the room. "I'm here to get the tray." She moved toward the table, only sending a slight glance in his direction, causing a light blush to stain her cheeks.

"Bonnie, wait," he said. "Come here." He slipped over a little and patted the edge of the bed. "Please talk to me."

She stopped and turned, looking at the foot of his bed.

"Please. I won't bite. I promise."

She moved slowly over to the side of the bed and tentatively sat on its edge.

He reached out, took her hand in his, and felt her tremble. She tried to pull back, but he gently held onto her hand.

"I want to thank you for all your help."

"It's…it was nothing," she murmured.

He squeezed her hand. "Look at me."

She raised her eyes and met his. His smile was easy and even, his eyes bright. She felt like she could fall into those golden eyes. Like a magnet, they held her gaze.

He studied her face. Her eyes were dark green, a color he'd never seen before. Against her creamy skin and surrounded by her wavy dark hair, they held a depth he wanted to explore. He swallowed and wondered if she'd felt his pulse quicken.

A slight frown creased her brow.

"Don't worry. What you are sensing is a very natural reaction to you."

Her cheeks pinkened even more.

His pulse slowed. She knew she hadn't done it and looked at him.

"When I was in college," he explained, "we did studies on regulating our pulse and heartbeat. I guess because of what was happening in my brain, I couldn't do it. I've never met anyone who could calm someone as much as you do. Your voice compelled me to follow it."

He thinks it was my voice. She smiled for the first time. At least she didn't have to explain things—at least not yet.

"Looks like I'm going to be around for a while. I'd like to see more of you."

"Mike asked if I would help you. I mean, he wants me to be there so you can move around and I can steady you, if you need. But, if you can do it yourself, you don't need my help."

"What I'm trying to say, and I'm obviously not doing a very good job of it, is that I'd like to get to know you. I mean, if you want to."

Bonnie let it sink in before she nodded. She let her eyes meet his even though it made her blush. That same feeling she'd had in the elevator seemed to wrap around them. It took everything she had to break the mood. "Right now, I better get back to work." She stood. "I'm glad you're better." She walked over to the table and picked up the tray he'd already loaded. As she got to the end of the bed. She looked at him. "I'd like to get to know you, too."

As she let herself out of the room, she glanced back to see him smile.

It took a moment for him to speak. Being near her enthralled him. "Tomorrow, then," he finally said.

"Rest well," she said and pulled the door closed behind her. Taking a deep breath, she felt her smile grow all the way down the hall.

Chapter Five

Ray had just finished texting with Gillian when a knock sounded on the door.

"Enter."

Mike stepped into the room. "Time for me to check out my patient. Any problems? Pain? Headache? Dizziness? Confusion? Fatigue?"

"No. Just tired. Bored."

Mike laughed as he took the blood pressure cuff out of his bag. "Well, plan on it for a few days." He took Ray's blood pressure, listened to his chest and back, listened to his carotid artery, used his pen light to check his eyes, then did a few simple neurological tests. "I want to check the femoral artery puncture area to make sure it's holding and healing."

Ray pushed down the covers, arched up, and pushed down his pajama bottoms while Mike got another bandage out of his bag. Mike removed the one covering the wound and looked for blood. Not a drop. The wound looked good, too. "Stand up for me. I want to make sure there's no bulge."

He swung his legs over and stood. Mike watched the site, giving it a few seconds while the blood flow changed. "Looks good. Lie back down and I'll dress it."

Ray leaned back against the pillows and watched Mike apply some cream and the bandage. "When can I get up? I mean more than to sit at the table to eat?"

"If you are feeling good tomorrow, after lunch, I don't see why you can't go sit on the porch for a little bit. I'm holding off because I know if you go to the dining room, you will be inundated with well-wishers. Ruthorford is one of the most caring places, but they are also a curious bunch. They will drive you to distraction, and right now, I want you resting."

Ray grimaced, making Mike smile. "However, I have a therapist I think you will like. In fact, it should be right up your alley. You'll meet her tomorrow. Tonight, get some sleep. I'll check on you in the morning. Early. Doctor time. If you are still looking this good, I'll put on a waterproof bandage so you and do more than a sponge bath. Carefully, mind you. You don't want to pop that artery plug. You could bleed out."

"I'm heading to the kitchen. You want anything?" Mike asked.

"No. Teresa left me some drinks and ice. I think I'll get some rest. Thanks, Doc."

"It's Mike. You take care. You've got your phone. Teresa put my direct dial in it. You were pretty full, so she put it on 9."

"Thanks, Mike. Please tell everyone else thanks, too."

"Oh, I'm sure you'll get a chance. Sooner or later, they'll all drop by."

Teresa walked out of the dining room as Mike stepped into the lobby. "How is he?" she asked.

"A lot better than I let on. Thanks to Sim, the plug is sealed. I just don't want to tempt fate. I wish I could get Sim in to do a scan, but…." He let the thought drift off.

"How about Morgan?"

"Or her, but how?"

"You let me worry about that. You done?"

"And then some," he said, setting his bag on the counter and pulling her into his arms.

Before he could take the kiss much deeper, she pulled back. "Aby's been asking for her daddy." She nodded her head toward the dining room.

He frowned. "She's up awfully late."

"And having a wonderful time, holding court." She put her arm through his and led him toward the sound of his daughter's laughter.

***

Ray's eyes opened. The room was dark. The only light was the glow from the small lights in the willow by the creek that filtered into the room. He heard voices. Not close. One he recognized well. It was that sultry low tone that drove him nuts.

"I can't. I don't want to impose."

"You like him. He likes you. You aren't imposing. Just take the breakfast tray to him and stay while he eats. I'm sure he'll enjoy the company."

He wasn't sure who was talking, but he knew the one they were talking to was Bonnie. Were they in the hall?

He heard a door close and the sound of water running, muffling the voices. He rose up on his arm and concentrated.

"He's an outsider. There's no future. No reason to hope."

"You like him. That's enough reason to hope. It's a conversation, not a wedding."

Ray smiled, picturing Bonnie blushing. Then, too many noises interfered. He got up and walked into the bathroom, turning on the water. He stepped back at the sound. It was loud. He yawned, popping his ears. And listened. The tinnitus, that constant static he'd finally grown accustomed to, was gone. Tentatively, he opened his mouth and tightened his jaw, half afraid it would return. Nope. He knocked on the counter. Loud. He knocked softly. Better but still pronounced.

Crawling back into bed, he listened. He heard voices and doors closing. He heard a whistle in the distance and a bird call in response to the whistle. Finally, putting the other pillow over the side of his head, he drifted off.

He was up when Mile knocked on the door. Ray announced that his tinnitus was gone even before Mike had closed the door.

"But," Ray added, "it's like my hearing is super sharp. I thought I heard talking outside my room last night, but then I heard other things. I think I could hear voices in the restaurant or something."

"But no ringing in your ears?"

"It was more like static. But, no. Not at all. But even my own voice is really loud."

"Hyperacusis," Mike said, pulled out an otoscope, and looked in both ears. "They look healthy. We'll do an audiology test. In the meantime," he said and reached in his bag, pulling out a small sealed cellophane bag, "these might help." He handed Ray the bag.

Ray took it and looked at Mike.

"Ear plugs."

Ray laughed. "Is there anything you don't have in that bag?"

"Not much. However, I got these because they've been working on the stage the town over, and I picked some up for the crew."

Ray held out his hand. "I don't want to—"

Mike pulled out another two bags. "Not a problem."

Finishing his exam, Mike stated, "Just make sure your ears are dry before you put the earplugs in."

"I will. Thanks."

***

Ray'd finished his shower and had just slipped on his jeans when the knock sounded. Suspecting it might be Bonnie, he called out, "Come on in."

She opened the door carrying a tray and almost dropped it when she spotted him emerging from the bathroom, bare-chested, his chest still damp, with low-slung jeans hugging his hips.

He stepped forward and took the tray, chuckling. "Whoa, girl. Don't want to lose this. I'm hungry. He set it on the table. "I'll just grab a shirt while you set up. I hope you brought some coffee for yourself."

Bonnie busied herself, setting up his plate, not answering. She was too flustered. She doubted she would ever forget the sight of his stomach muscles and the light sprinkling of blonde hair disappearing into his jeans. She almost knocked over the juice glass. She took a deep breath and stepped back just as he came around the table.

He took her arm, kept her from running into him, and steadied her. She looked around, and his eyes locked with hers. He smiled and guided her to the chair across from him. She sat, staring into his eyes.

When he took the seat across from her, he looked at the omelet. "Looks great. I hear you sing like an angel."

She felt the red moving up her neck. "Well, not quite like an angel," she said, and a smile quirked up the corner of her lips, thinking of how Claire teased her about having a siren's voice.

"Well, we do have something in common. You like to sing. I like to listen."

This time she really did smile. She noticed the bag of earplugs on the table and looked up at him.

He swallowed the egg and took a sip of coffee. "Ear plugs. I had tinnitus," he said, "ringing in the ears," he added at her frown. "Last night, it disappeared. I keep waiting for it to return. But everything suddenly seems so loud. Mike left these for me."

Her thoughts immediately went to Sim and his hyper hearing and Eryk, whose hearing wasn't as strong as Sim's, but was a lot more than others. Descendant traits. "You didn't have this before?" she said, keeping her voice soft.

"No. God, I love your voice," he added without thinking. "I'm sorry. I just find it so soothing."

"Thank you." She felt that cocoon weave around her. She forced herself to stay calm. This was her chance to find out some things for the descendants. She never thought of herself as a descendant, although she was one. "Where are you from?"

"D.C. Well, actually, Georgetown. My parents are both professors at George Washington University. I live in Alexandria now."

"What do they teach?"

"Mom's in cultural anthropology and dad's all IT."

"Wouldn't his mom love to get her mitts on Ruthorford?" Bonnie thought and forced her mind back to the man across from her. She laughed. "Wow. That must make for some interesting dinner table conversations."

"You have no idea." He poured more coffee and took a drink. "I do love this coffee."

"It's a special blend that Bill concocted. That was Teresa's first husband. He passed away a little while ago."

"The little girl?"

"Aby. That's Mike and Teresa's. Long story and not mine to tell, but Aby is the jewel of everyone's eye. A late-life miracle. They are so happy."

"Mike's an incredible doctor," Ray said

She nodded. "He is." She turned the conversation back to him. "What do you do?"

"I design book covers," he said simply. "Dad's kinda pleased that I discovered digital art at this late stage. He actually helped me. When I got long Covid, my hands started shaking and became unsteady. But I could operate a trackball. Dad introduced me to the world of digital art. I take pictures, then transform them into covers for my clients."

"We have a bookstore," she said. "I wonder if your covers are there."

"We'll have to walk over and see some time."

Bonnie noticed he'd finished eating. She nodded as she stood. "I have to get back, and you need to rest." She started stacking his empty plates on the tray. "You can keep the coffee if you like."

He picked up the tray before she could and followed her to the door. "Do you think we could have a meal where we are both eating sometime?"

She turned, took the tray, and smiled at him. "I'd like that."

"I'll see you later, Bonnie. Thanks for talking to me."

With a simple nod, she moved into the hall, and he closed the door. Then, he heard the soft humming. Sultry didn't begin to describe it. "Damn, what a voice," he said, half to himself.

Bonnie carried the tray to the kitchen and set it on the counter, waiting for Teresa to come into the kitchen. She didn't have long to wait.

"Well, did you have a good time?"

"Very much. I also learned some things. He had tinnitus before he came here, probably due to Covid. Now his hearing has become really sensitive, and the tinnitus is gone."

"Do you think it has to do with what you or Sim did?"

"It would have to be Sim if anyone. Not me. I just calm the pulse and blood pressure."

Teresa raised a single brow.

"No. That is all I do. Anyway, his parents teach at George Washington University. He was born in Georgetown. Maybe that will help with his background."

"That's great. I will let Jenn know. What do you think?"

"I think he is what he is. Did Mike do his blood type?"

"I'm sure. He hasn't said, so I'm guessing it isn't RH null, like ours."

"Honestly, I hope not."

"Why?"

"I don't know. There's something about descendant men that's so…so much."

Teresa patted her arm. "I know exactly what you mean. They are incredible and wonderful, but they are descendants. We descendant women; however, we're just perfect."

Bonnie chuckled. "Yeah. Perfect."

Chapter Six

"Gillian," he laughed into the phone. "I'm fine. Better, in fact." He absently adjusted the earplug against her high voice. "In fact. I would appreciate the distraction. They won't let me do anything, and I'm ready to scream." He heard a knock on the door. "Hang on, Gillian. Come in," he called out. "Let me call you back. Just send the changes to my email. I will get to it immediately. No. I'm fine. I promise. I'll call you once I look over what you want. Give my love to Patti."

Looking at the gorgeous redhead standing inside the door, he absently hung up. "I know you. Wait. The Shoppe of Spells." He thought for a moment. "I'm sorry I don't remember your name."

"Morgan." She flashed him a smile meant to melt any heart. It worked; he just looked at her. "I'm here to break you out," she said, moving forward.

"Seriously?" he asked, excited even if it was just down the hall. He had already swung his feet over the side of the bed. He was definitely going stir-crazy.

She stepped over and held out her hand, lowering her lashes. When he took her hand, she looked at him, stepping back as if to guide him, and scanned him from head to toe.

He stared at her. Her irises looked like they'd taken on a swirling motion.

"How are you feeling?" she said, turning away.

"Really good," he responded as she released his hand.

"If you don't have a lightweight jacket, I think we can find one for you."

"In the closet," he said and walked to the sliding doors in the hall separating the bedroom from the bath. He pulled out a light jacket and turned back, looking at her eyes. They were a beautiful bright green. No swirling. It crossed his mind to tell Mike, but he was soon distracted by the freedom of walking down the hall.

He started to turn toward the dining room when Morgan took his arm. "Nope. We're headed outside."

"Really?" Ray asked and flashed her a big smile, making her laugh.

"You really are stir-crazy. Don't get too excited." She walked to the door. He stepped around her and pulled open the outer door.

"We're only going to sit on the porch," she said and led him to a pair of oversized black rocking chairs turned to the side, facing down Main Street. He sat in the one nearest the porch rail, and she took the one next to him. It looked like a wonderland of orange, gold, and brown colors, with some red and purple thrown in. Not a window, door, or lamppost had been spared.

"Teresa said you all do this in a day."

"Pretty much. There will be the odds and ends added, but the majority of the decorations go up in a day. We learned it worked out better that way. You missed the dinner. I'm sorry. We always have a huge dinner the night of the decorating, plus Teresa keeps refreshments on the buffet all day for people to stop by."

"Well, my hat's off to everyone. It's amazing."

"It takes a lot of planning. Teresa's one master planner. Would you like some tea or coffee? Or hot chocolate? With marshmallows." She stood.

"I'd love some hot chocolate. Hold the marshmallows." He watched her go back inside and took out his phone to snap pictures. When he turned it to the side to capture the gingerbread house across from the Bed & Breakfast, a petite cherub of a woman waved. He waved back.

"That's our Post Mistress, Brenda," Morgan said, stepping back to the chairs and handing him a cup.

"That's the quaintest Post Office I've ever seen."

"Apparently, that house had many iterations until Miss Brenda took over. She's been doing that long before I came."

He looked at her. "You're not from around here?"

She shook her head. "Long story."

"I'm not going anywhere." He took a sip of the most decadent hot chocolate he'd ever had and licked the froth from his upper lip.

"Okay," Morgan acquiesced. "I was born and raised in Virginia."

"Where?"

"Williamsburg."

"I love Colonial Williamsburg. Been there many times. Sorry. Go on."

"I got a letter from a lawyer informing me my parents were dead and I'd inherited one half of a shop. Talk about panic. I had no idea I'd been adopted. I came here and met Dorian, who is NOT my brother, by the way. He'd been a ward of my birth parents and had inherited the other half. We met. I fell head over heels, and the rest is history."

"Your adoptive parents? They never told you?"

"No. Again, long story. They were planning on telling me but hadn't gotten around to it. They were on a trip when I got the letter from the lawyer. I was terrified they were the ones who'd been killed. I was so relieved when I reached them. Still, a shock like that takes some getting used to. I realize now just how lucky I am. They are incredible. You'll meet them next week at the Thanksgiving feast."

"Next week is Thanksgiving?"

"Uh-huh. Oh, good. Di's coming up the sidewalk, and she's carrying a big box. You are in for a treat."

He watched as the young woman approached the building with a determined step and a smile. As she came up the steps, he could smell cinnamon. He tilted his head. "You look familiar."

"We almost met the day you arrived. I came in, then left, having forgotten something."

"Ahh. That's why I thought I'd seen you before."

Di opened the box and held it in front of him. Resting on paper were two bear claws covered in cinnamon.

He took one.

Morgan took the other and immediately took a big bite. "Oh, Di, these are so good."

Ray made sounds and nodded vigorously, making Di laugh. "I'll take that as approval."

He nodded again.

"Let me take these in, and I'll be right back. You and I have some business to do," she said to Ray.

The confection stopped midway to his mouth.

"Oh, I do so love intrigue. But you shouldn't keep him from enjoying his treat," Morgan said and stood. "I'll take these to your mom for you. You can have my seat."

"Thanks." She took the rocking chair next to Ray, sitting forward so it didn't rock.

"Your mom?"

"I'm Diane Ruthorford. Di to my friends. Teresa's my mother."

"I'm Ray Grissom," he said, dusted the sugar off his hand, and held it out.

She took it in a firm grip. "Oh, I know who you are. But I knew you by a different name. Why the name change, Luke?

He didn't seem surprised that he was recognized. "You probably know about my stroke. After Covid, when I lost some use of my hand, I started doing digital art covers and decided to use a different name. Things would have gotten...," he hesitated, before continuing, "let's say they might have gotten difficult for my clients if people knew who I was."

She nodded. "I can see that. I've admired your art."

He swallowed some hot chocolate, washing down the rest of the pastry. "You're an artist?"

"I'm an art therapist."

Ray unconsciously looked down at his hands.

"Mike contacted KC, and she contacted me. I met with Mike this morning. I realized I hadn't seen any of your work in a few years and—"

"KC?" He interrupted her. "The KC?"

Di loved seeing his expression and laughed, pointing to the building right across from the Bed & Breakfast, next to the Fashion Flare, where he'd met Claire. "That's The Art Gallery. KC runs it. She has a couple of your pieces there."

"I have a couple of hers," he said. "Wow. I can't believe she's here. I mean right there." He pointed and reminded Di of a kid who'd learned Santa lived in town.

"If you behave, I'll introduce you," she teased, laughing. "I think I'll introduce you anyway since you reminded me of Morgan's twins at Christmas."

She saw him shiver and stood. "Time to get you inside."

"I don't wanna," he whined and pouted, a twinkle in his eyes.

"Now you do sound like the twins."

He stepped around her and opened the door, giving her a megawatt smile.

"We'll start in the morning. I'll bring supplies."

"I have a laptop and trackball."

"And I have pencils and paper. We want to use that hand. See what it can do."

"You're right," he said, a sad note in his voice. "I haven't produced anything in quite a while."

"I understand you've been creating some pretty phenomenal book covers. I'd like to see some."

"They're on my computer."

"How about 10 a.m. tomorrow?"

"Sounds good." He stopped in the lobby.

"Nope. You are to go back and rest. I don't want to be responsible for a relapse."

"I have a feeling you're going to be a hard taskmaster."

She laughed. "You've no idea," she said and turned toward the sound of Teresa's voice.

"I thought I heard my daughter's voice. I see you two have met." Teresa walked over and hugged Di, keeping her arm around her when she turned to Ray. "I hear she's going to help you. You couldn't get anyone better. But I'm prejudiced."

Teresa studied him. "You look a little pale. You okay?"

"Yeah. Maybe a little tired."

"Why don't you go rest? I'll send a tray down in about an hour or so. Want something to drink?"

"Nope. You stocked that mini fridge. I'm good."

They watched him go down the hall and listened for the door to close. Teresa led Di into the dining room to her table. "Do you think he knew you?"

"Not at all. Of course, my being your daughter helps. Plus, with Diane Ruthorford not known in the art world, I think I'm good. I think I can help him."

"Gillian indicated that he seems to love what he does now. She met him at a book signing. It was held in a small art gallery. He happened to be there. They met at the luncheon. He picked up her book and made some suggestions on the cover. She jokingly said if he ever decided to make a career move to call her. A few months later, her phone rang. Gillian said he was upfront with her, saying he was having some trembling issues and was trying to do some digital art. He asked her if she would take a chance on him. He's done three covers, a banner, and some artwork for her. It seems to have worked out for both of them."

"I just hate that he feels he had to give up what he did."

"Do you regret losing Deirdre Silvermane?"

Di shook her head. "Sadly, being a renowned artist wasn't my calling. It was a tool honed and used for the government. The fact that I enjoyed it was a boon. But I knew him. Art was his passion. Have you ever seen his work?"

"No."

"Come on. I want you to see what I'm talking about." She grabbed Teresa's hand and dragged her out the door. They crossed the street just as KC was coming out the front door.

"Don't lock it. I'll do it."

"Hey. What's up?"

"I want Mom to see Luke's work."

"Ray," Teresa corrected. "Let's respect his wishes."

"Of course. You're right, Mom," Di said, remembering how she'd felt.

Teresa gave her hand a squeeze, making Di smile.

KC opened the door, holding it. I want to see her see it," she said and followed them inside, hitting the lights. I put it on the right corridor, toward the back. I didn't know if he'd want it front and center."

"You should ask him yourself. When he learned you had the gallery, he was like a kid waiting to see Santa. He would go nuts if you showed up." She led Teresa around the hallway and stopped in front of a deep-set canvas.

"Oh, wow."

"It's a mixed-media masterpiece. The use of color and materials gives it a true three-dimensional effect. It looks like you could step right into that sunset. It's an unusual use of color. One I've never seen done before, but it works. It grabs you and won't let go."

Teresa stepped to the side. Then back. There was something about it. She pulled out her phone and hit a number. "Sim. Can you come to the gallery for a moment?"

She looked at the screen, smiled, and hung up before tuning to Di, who was frowning. "He's on his way."

No more than she'd finished than the door opened, and Sim rushed in with a quick whistle, his fingers starting to sign the moment he saw them.

"No, Sim, we're fine," Di said as she walked over and, rising on tiptoe, kissed him. No matter how long they were together, if he walked into a room where she was, her heart sped up, and her body felt a vibration.

"Sim, I want you to look at this and tell me what you see," Teresa said.

Sim turned and looked at the display she pointed to. His brows furrowed as he stepped forward. He blinked and looked again. He turned to her and started signing. *I've never seen anything like this. His use of color and the mix is such*

that it affects the color spectrum I can see on my other level.
When he turned to them, his eyes were swirling. He blinked
and his eyes returned to normal. *He created this using
tetrachromatic vision. You can't see what I see. Or what he
created. But what makes it so unique is how he did it. This
comes as close to giving you a sense of what we see as I've
ever seen. It's phenomenal.*

"Do you think he's a descendant?" KC asked.

"The bloodwork doesn't indicate it, but it's not final.
We're waiting on the genetic analysis."

"I think I'd like to meet him," KC said. "What time are
you going tomorrow? She asked Di.

"I'll stop by here tomorrow on my way. I need to pick
up some supplies, anyway."

***

Bonnie stepped into the kitchen carrying Ray's tray,
which had been barely touched. "I don't like the way he
looks. I pulled the bed tray out of the closet and set it up over
the bed. He said he was just tired and asked me to sit and talk
to him. He said my voice was soothing. Can you make sure
Mike checks on him? I'm a little concerned."

"Did you ask him if anything was bothering him?"

"I did. He said nothing in particular. Said he has a
headache. When I walked over to take the tray, I leaned over
and felt his forehead. No fever. I put my hand on his shoulder
for a moment. His pulse was a little high, but the blood
pressure seemed low. I didn't try to regulate it. I want Mike
to look at him."

Teresa was already on the phone, talking to Mike. She hung up. "He's on his way." She saw the frown on Bonnie's face and pulled her into a hug. "He'll be okay. He's in the best place he can be." She gave Bonnie a little push and allowed herself to remote view what Bonnie saw in Ray's room. He looked very lethargic.

"He's wearing those earplugs, yet he could hear me so easily," Bonnie said and turned away, wiping down the counter.

"Have you eaten?" When Bonnie just shook her head, she went over, dished up some French Onion Soup, and put it on a tray with a baguette. "Take this and go sit at my table and eat. I'll be out in a few minutes."

When Mike walked into the dining room, coming from the hallway, it startled Bonnie. She'd been watching the lobby. He must have come over immediately. She stood. "I'll get you something to eat."

"Not right now. I'm going back to the clinic. I want to get these blood samples run. Where's Teresa?"

Before Bonnie could say kitchen, Teresa appeared. She walked over and gave Mike a kiss. "You're fast."

"That I am. Listen, I need you to do me a favor. I want you to go in and check on him, give him a little push."

"Of course," she said and waited for him to continue.

"He's negative for Covid. His BP is 97 over 58, but his pulse is 86. I took some blood. I'm taking it back now. His eyes look good, his wound is almost healed, but he is extremely lethargic, even though he's trying not to be. He admitted feeling this way after he was finally getting over Covid the first time." Mike shook his head. "We just don't know enough about this virus. What it does to different bodies is so complex and varied. I'm so damned glad descendants seem to be immune."

"And you're as vaccinated as we can get you, and we keep giving you energy," Teresa said, putting her arm around her husband.

"Knock on wood," Bonnie said and tapped her head.

Mike smiled and turned to her, "You doing okay, little girl?"

She nodded.

"He'll be okay. I have an idea. Let me get this to the clinic." He leaned over and kissed Teresa. "I love you."

"I love you, too. I'll check on Ray in a few moments."

***

Teresa knocked on the door and let herself in. "You decent?" She asked, a lilt in her voice. "Mike wanted me to make sure you had a fresh pitcher of water.

She watched him struggle to push himself up on the pillows. "Did I wake you?" she asked.

He thought for a moment. "I don't think so. I don't know why I'm so tired. I only sat on the porch for a few moments."

"Maybe a few moments too long," she said and set the pitcher on the bedside table, unwrapped a glass, and poured some water. "Here, drink some of this. We have the most fabulous spring in Ruthorford."

As he took the glass, he touched her fingers, and the fatigue seeped through her.

After he'd taken a couple sips of water, she took the glass from him. "As you will learn, I play momma to all the youngins here in Ruthorford, no matter their age. You are gonna be no different." She tilted his face up to hers and looked into his eyes. Then, she made a play of feeling his forehead and let her hands run down his arms until she had hold of his hands. "Is anything bothering you?" she asked, distracting him as she sent a gentle push into his body through his hands. "You can trust me. Anything that might be worrying you?"

"Not really," he shook his head and shuddered as the energy moved through him. "Had you asked me a while back, I would have given you a list, but I felt so much better today, I really had hoped I was getting over this crap."

"And you will." She gave his hands a reassuring squeeze, adding another push, and watched his color return to his cheeks. She reached over and handed him the glass. "Drink some more before I leave."

He took a couple of swallows and looked at the glass, frowning. "That must be some spring. I really do feel better."

"Good. You get some sleep. Mike will probably check on you again before he heads to bed."

"Thank you—all of you—for your kindnesses. I really do appreciate it."

"Have you talked to your parents? We didn't call since you were doing so well. I didn't want to scare them."

"I called them yesterday. They are both getting ready for exams—they are professors—so I told them not to worry and that I'd call them and keep them informed."

"Good. Get some sleep." She let herself out of the room.

Chapter Seven

Mike stepped into the tea room, closed the door after him, and pulled down the shade, which had Closed on the other side. He turned around to see a large contingent of the descendants there. "Thank you for coming so early. I figured it would be better to meet away from the Bed & Breakfast since I have no idea how strong Ray's hearing is."

"We don't have an issue. They're feeding us," Eryk said, taking a large bite of the breakfast croissant stuffed with eggs, sausage, and cheese.

Jasmine crinkled her nose. "Said the bottomless pit that I married."

Jenn popped up from where she was sitting with her husband, John. "Hey, Uncle Mike," she said and gave him a kiss on the cheek.

Mike hugged her. Seeing her bouncy blonde curls, it was sometimes hard for him to remember that his niece was the head of The Abbott House Foundation and their top lawyer. One of the few "outsiders" to be allowed to be a part of the descendants' group, she had been thrown into the midst of their challenges from the get-go. "Hey, squirt. When are you and John going to come have dinner with us?"

"How about tonight? I'm taking the day off and dragging John around with me to see everyone."

"That's great. John, thank you for coming as the Native American council rep. I want us all to be on the same page." John nodded.

"I hear we have a long-term visitor," Ozzy said. He was the most recent descendant to find his way to Ruthorford.

"Unlike you, Ray has no descendant traits. He is a true outsider. But, he needs our help."

"What's up? I thought he was doing well," Dorian asked.

"It's the damned virus, I'm almost positive. Even though he's testing negative, I think it's done some damage to his body. But, given the reaction he's having to Teresa's pushes of energy, I think Sim might be able to help him, if everyone agrees."

Sim, signed, *I'm in. I spent some time connected to this man. He is definitely worth helping.*

"I have an idea," Mike said. "We might be able to do this without compromising your privacy. I want Sim to pretend to do some TENS treatments. That stands for Transcutaneous Electrical Nerve Stimulation. Looks like the outside world may be catching up to some of the things descendants do, except they need machines." He laughed and looked around the room at the people he knew, admired, and loved. "Since this technology is something we can explain to Ray, we're going to let him think that's what's going on, except Sim's really going to be using his talent to help Ray."

Sim says Ray has, or had, tetrachromacy, an extra cone in his eyes, which gives him vision similar to Sim's. Di says he was a renowned artist before suffering consequential medical conditions following Covid. Those conditions took away his enhanced vision, gave him constant headaches, tinnitus, and weakness and trembling in his hands, primarily his left, which is his dominant hand.

"Poor man," Jasmine said. "Mike, you keep up with your boosters, you hear."

"Not everyone has the same reactions. Hell, it seems reactions to the virus are unpredictable, at best. And, yes, I am up to date on the vaccines. Plus, with all the damned pushes you all give me, I'm surprised I don't glow in the dark. But, I do feel they help."

"Back to Ray. I think the clot we found was a consequence of the virus, but I don't think he had a previous stroke. Once we removed the clot, his condition improved. His hands have stopped trembling. The tinnitus is gone, but he now has hyperacusis, which may or may not be correctable. Unfortunately, his body is weakening. I've run every test I can think of and can't find any reason. We know the virus can hide and affect systems on the smallest level." He ran his fingers through his hair in frustration. "Damn, there's so much we just don't know. If nothing else, maybe Sim's efforts can forestall or negate what is happening."

Ozzy spoke up. "I think I may have something you can use to simulate the equipment. Of course, it won't do anything, but it will give Sim a cover."

Jenn frowned. "I hate to be the wet blanket here, but what about his informed consent?"

"Well, considering this is experimental, we can cover it with that. We don't know the risks or guarantees. We are trying to possibly save his life." Mike's voice had an edge to it.

"I want to be present when you talk to him," Jenn insisted.

"Not a problem. The crux of the matter is he needs intervention, sooner rather than later. I don't think turning him over to the outside will help him. I do think it could kill him. Truthfully, we may be his only chance. Now, it's up to you." He stopped when his phone rang.

He listened. "I'll be right there." He put his phone away. "Looks like we are going to have to move even faster. He's not doing well." He headed to the door.

Sim got up and took Mike's arm, nodding. Ozzy stood. "I'm running by the house and will bring something with me. Sim, just go with the flow."

"I need to be there to protect you all, as well as him," Jess said.

"Go," John said. "We have never turned down helping someone." He looked around the room. Nods of agreement spread through the room.

"Thank you," Mike said and ran out the door with Jenn and Sim on his heels.

When he ran into the room, having grabbed his bag from behind the counter, Bonnie was standing next to the bed.

"How are you doing?" Mike asked Ray.

"Not so good." His voice was weak.

"Bonnie, I want you to stabilize him. Sim, counter her." Mike prayed Sim understood what he was asking.

Bonnie reached over and put both hands on his arm, afraid one wouldn't be enough. She'd given him little adjustments, elevating his pulse rate to hers, but she was afraid to do more without Mike there, and it hadn't been enough. Now, she sought, but barely found, a pulse. As soon as Sim touched his shoulder on the other side, she felt the blood pressure right itself and the pulse stabilize. She knew it wasn't her.

With another slow push of energy, Sim stepped back so Mike could take his blood pressure, and check his pulse and oxygen, as well as his lungs and heart.

While Mike worked, Ozzy stepped into the room, carrying a device. Mike looked at Ozzy and nodded. Ray's eyes had brightened, and he seemed more alert.

"Ray, I'm Ozzy Henderson. I live here and am President of the technical division of CDI. We have been working with The Abbott House Foundation," he gave a nod toward Jenn, who had taken her place at the foot of the bed, "on a device to generate and send electromagnetic energy into the body. I believe it could help you. Sim is trained and would be your therapist."

Mike had finished and helped Ray sit up. He definitely looked more alert.

Ozzy saw Ray looking at his prosthesis. Ray held out his arm. This was one of our first collaborative efforts," he said. "Since I was in no position to have delays, the color is a bit off, but, minus a few rather *humorous* initial events, pun intended, I will be forever grateful."

"That's pretty amazing. Hey, I'm game," Ray said. "What have I got to lose?"

Jenn spoke up. "Ray, I'm an attorney, as well as the head of The Abbott Foundation, but I want to be certain you know what you are agreeing—"

Ray interrupted her. "Listen. I've had more help here than I had in years. If I hadn't come, I've no doubt I would be dead, or worse. I don't know what is happening to me, but it's not good. If these people are willing to try and help me, I'm all in. This is my verbal agreement. Get the papers you want created and I'll sign, but I want to start as soon as possible. I am tired of having crisis after crisis. And, honestly, I'm scared shitless."

All eyes turned to Jenn. "It's not like he doesn't have enough witnesses," she said. "I will draw up papers, but you have my okay if you want to get started. "I'll get out of your way. Nice meeting you, Ray."

Ozzy set the box on the end of the bed and pulled out a mat, some wires, wristbands, and a small machine. "The mat will go under your back. The connections will go to the machine and to the wristbands. That way, Sim can direct where and how much is delivered."

Sim started signing, but Ray held up his hand. "I don't know sign language," Ray said. "I'm sorry."

Sim looked at Bonnie. "Sim is non-verbal," she said. "He said that he would like to start tonight. For the next couple of days, he will come three times a day, reducing it as you improve."

Ray looked at Bonnie. "I'm going to need you to be here so I can understand what Sim is saying. However, I don't want to be a burden on you or your job. It's up to you," he finished.

She smiled at him. "I would be honored to be your interpreter," she said. "I'm sure Teresa would want me to help."

Bonnie stepped back as Ozzy helped Sim position the mat under Ray, attach the leads to the machine and to the wrist bands, then put the bands around Sim's wrists. Ozzy moved to the foot of the bed and turned on the machine. A green light glowed.

Sim signed to Bonnie. She immediately switched sides with Sim. She looked at Ray. "Sim wants to start with your left hand. Has it started trembling again at all?"

"No."

"Try not to show a reaction. It's me, Sim." The words formed in Bonnie's mind, and her eyes grew wide. But, as directed, she didn't turn toward Sim but stared wide-eyed at Ray.

"What's wrong?" Ray asked.

She swallowed and forced her voice lower and softer, feeling as though she would squeal if she spoke normally right now. "I just noticed that your left and right arms are slightly different, pulse-wise."

"Good save," Sim's voice filled her mind. *"I'm going to ask you some questions. You can think the answers and I will hear them in my mind."*

"Okay," she thought. To Ray, she said, "Why don't you close your eyes. Try to relax. It might help."

"Thanks. That was exactly what I was going to suggest." She felt the words and the chuckle that followed.

"You didn't ask me to?"

"Nope. But I want to scan him, and he might not like seeing my eyes."

"I'll keep watch." She glanced at Sim to see him open his eyes as they took on that swirling look. Yep, she definitely didn't want Ray to see that.

"I felt that," Sim replied.

"Oops."

Sim scanned Ray's body slowly, lingering around his neck and head, then moving back down, hesitating at the femoral artery puncture, before moving all the way down his body, then back up. He closed his eyes and opened them again, nodding to Mike.

He moved back. As soon as he did, Ray opened his eyes. Sim started signing. *I am going to give energy and massage the hand. Then I am going the hold both arms and let the energy flow through you. You should sleep like a baby.*

Bonnie repeated what he'd signed.

"Okay," Ray said. "So far, I just feel some warmth."

Sim signed again, *You might feel some tingling this time.*

Again, Bonnie told Ray what Sim had said.

"I'm good," Ray said.

While Sim worked, he sent a thought into Bonnie's mind. *"Please keep this method of communication between us. Not everyone knows I can do it. But, I want to be able to direct you if I need your help without stopping to sign."*

"Okay." Then, added. *"Thanks for trusting me."*

"Always," Sim's word was like a caress.

Sim stepped back and signed. *"That's good for tonight."*

As Bonnie interpreted, Ozzy moved forward to help lift Ray up, remove the pad, and help put pillows behind him. Ozzy took the pad and contacts and put everything back in the box.

"That was fast," Ray said.

Sim signed and Bonnie spoke. "We're starting out small. I'll increase it, depending on how you do."

"Nice meeting you, Ray. I hope this helps," Ozzy said,

"I think it already has. I don't feel quite as fuzzy-headed."

"Terrific. I'll see you tomorrow."

"Thanks so much."

Mike stepped over and attached the blood pressure cuff.

"I'm going to go get you some fresh breakfast," Bonnie said, looking at the tray that had been long forgotten. "I'll be right back." She picked up the tray she'd left on the table when she'd found him listless earlier and left.

Mike walked into the dining room as Bonnie came out of the kitchen with a tray. "I'm taking this to Ray while he's still awake. Everyone is upstairs. There are pastries up there, too." She grinned, knowing how he loved Di's pastries.

As she walked past him, she stopped. "In case no one has told you lately, you are awesome." She flashed a big smile and headed through the lobby.

"Thank you, Bonnie. That means a lot." He put his bag in its location behind the counter, just in case, and stepped into the elevator. It was quiet until he stepped off on the fourth floor and heard voices in the library.

He entered the library and Ozzy handed him a mug of coffee as he made his way to the couch.

"Just what the hell was that thing you improvised?" He asked Ozzy.

"Well, the pad is from a massage thing I ordered, and the device is something I developed with Jim at the lab to measure resistance and potential for my prosthesis."

"I'll be damned. It looked authentic to me," Mike said, chugging coffee. "What's your take, Sim?"

Sim flashed a big grin and signed, *Yeah. Looked pretty real to me, too.*

Mike caught his smile and shook his head. "Smartass. I meant on Ray's condition."

Sim lifted a brow before signing. *The puncture wound looks great. Didn't see any obstruction anywhere. His aura is clear but not as vibrant as it should be. Whatever that virus did to him, if it was the virus, it was sneaky. His nerves look good. His brain doesn't have any cloudy spots. There is no way I can know if his cones have been affected. I don't know if one is damaged or if that would affect his tetrachromacy. I also don't think anything I do will affect his hyperacusis. I don't know if a non-descendant can control it like we can. I suggest letting me send energy through him three times a day for a week and then re-evaluate.*

"Damn, Sim. I think that's the longest speech you've ever given," Mike said but held up his hand before Sim could shoot him the finger and laughed. "But I truly appreciate your thoroughness. I agree. Since you can get immediate feedback, I'll leave it to you to determine the intensity and duration. However, before you do the next treatment, I want to take him to the clinic and do some baseline tests. If I haven't said it, 'Thank you, Sim.' We are so lucky to have you."

Chapter Eight

Ray sat up in bed, looking out the window, wondering if, now that they all knew who he was, he should go back to his "normal" name, Luke. His mind returned to his art studio, the showings, marketing, and public appearances. In truth, the only part he missed was his art. He loved doing the book covers, but they were constrained to too many specifics for his creativity. He didn't miss the rest of it at all. Glancing at the trees in the distance and the vibrant colors he saw once more, then down at his hand, he decided to stick with Ray. After all, he'd never been comfortable promoting himself, although everyone said he was good at it.

Not like his friend, Diedre Silvermane. God, he missed her. Her death had devastated him, so much so he'd had to put the art he had of hers away. Maybe it was time to put them out again. The pain had eased, and when he thought of her it was without the pain. Funny, he'd thought of her more since he'd been in Ruthorford. Maybe that art gallery would have some of her work. He'd have to ask KC when he met her. His smile broadened. He couldn't wait to meet such a renowned artist.

A light knock on the door brought him back to the moment, and he realized he felt pretty good. A whole lot better, in fact, than he had before that troupe of people had manhandled him this morning.

"It's unlocked," he called out.

Mike and Bonnie stepped into the room. She wasn't averting her gorgeous eyes like she had been. When she smiled at him, it went straight to his heart.

"Hi," he said. "I don't know what you all did, but I feel a whole lot better."

"Good, then you won't mind taking a little trip," Mike said.

"Let me guess. The clinic. I'll go. Just let me—"

"No need to change," Mike interrupted him. "I want to put you through a few tests to set a baseline. I'd have liked to have done it before your first treatment, but I'm afraid the trip would have been done in an ambulance."

Ray looked at Bonnie.

"She's coming with us so she can drive you back. I really need to stay at the clinic."

"That's great. Maybe I can coerce her into driving me around a little before we come back here."

"Let's see how you feel after the tests." Bonnie's sexy chuckle had his eyes riveting on her. "You've never been subjected to Mike's idea of a 'few'." She made air quotes. "You'll feel like a horse who's been ridden hard and put up wet."

"I'm not that bad," Mike said. Before she could comment, he added, "Let's get this show on the road."

***

She'd been right. By the time they left, Ray wasn't sure he'd be awake by the time they got back. He'd had blood drawn, peed in a cup, spit in a vial, had his nose swabbed, and had three different physicians give him a physical. That didn't include the MRI, EKG, EEG, and EMG. He also had audiology and ophthalmology workups. Given everything they knew about him, he figured if he crapped out, they could just build another one.

He laid his head back against the headrest and closed his eyes.

"Told ya," Bonnie said.

He turned his head and looked at her, suddenly taken by her profile. She was gorgeous. She glanced over, smiling, her eyes sparkling. "Still want that tour?"

"All I want is a nap, and I hate naps."

"How about I get you back and bring you some lunch, then you can nap?"

"How about I nap first, then you bring food?"

She turned and looked at him. "Are you okay?"

"Seriously tired. But," he emphasized, "nothing like this morning. Just tired."

"All right. You nap for an hour, then I'll bring food. I'll talk with Sim about postponing the midday session."

"You're an angel."

Suddenly, Bonnie couldn't come up with some cute retort. It didn't matter; it looked like he'd drifted off, anyway.

***

By the time Sim showed, accompanied by Bonnie, Ray felt great. He wasn't sure if it had been the nap or that open-faced roast beef sandwich with mashed potatoes, smothered with gravy, and peas that had done it. He'd come close to damned near licking the plate.

Sim pulled up a chair beside Ray's bed and started signing. Bonnie, who'd moved to the other side of the bed, interpreted.

"Sim says the preliminary findings from some of the tests are good. You're hearing, which you probably suspect, is off the chart. He also has hyperacusis and has, over time, learned to control it internally," she said, glancing from Sim to Ray. "But he was born with it. It still can be annoying as hell, and he recommends earplugs and sound-canceling headphones. He will bring you some of his earplugs. They are better than the ones Mike gave you."

Sim looked at Bonnie before he started again, waiting for her to nod.

"You appear to have tetrachromacy, which is having one more cone than most people, giving you the ability to see more colors."

Ray interrupted. "Apparently, not anymore. I don't see the colors I used to."

"I sensed that having seen your original works and your book covers. Your eyes could have been damaged by the Covid virus. I can't tell you whether or not it will return. I'm hoping that this stimulation might help progress the healing. I am very sorry you have lost that. Your art is amazing."

Bonnie held up her hand, indicating she wanted to talk. "Sim has tetrachromacy," she said, "as do some of the women I've known." She was thinking of Morgan, specifically. She left out herself in the telling, affording her a look from Sim, so she added, "I understand it can be a blessing and a curse." She nodded to Sim once more.

"Wait," Ray said to Sim, "You have it?"

Sim nodded.

"So you can actually see my paintings like I created them."

Again, Sim nodded, then signed, his fingers moving very fast.

Bonnie rushed to catch up. "I can. I was fortunate to see it with Di, so I could ask her what she saw. Apparently, the way you did it appeals to all viewers."

Ray sat up, excited. "I've never talked to anyone who could see what I did."

Sim realized he had to be careful. The fact that he could switch his vision meant he could see both what Ray saw and what Di would see. Yet, he had a feeling his went even further. Still, he wanted to encourage Ray. He'd always believed confidence and faith helped in healing.

Sim looked at Bonnie, who nodded, speaking for Sim. "I have done some research on it. Truth be told, there is really no way to tell what we see once we see beyond the range that normal people see. There is little empirical evidence of males having it. It is suggested that it is sex-linked. Well, you and I are evidence that's not necessarily true. I believe it is a mutation. The fact that I can see the colors you projected in your art tells me you have it. And, if possible, I will do my best to help you have it again."

"Hell, if I could just have better use of my hand," Ray said, his voice rather sad, as he looked at his left hand.

"I am confident that you will regain full use of your hand." With that, Sim smiled and nodded.

"I wish I had your confidence."

Bonnie watched the interplay between the two men. At this point, her voice recited Sim's words. The men were talking as if she wasn't even there.

Sim started signing again. Bonnie spoke. "Your hand isn't trembling anymore, is it?"

Ray held out his hands, even and steady.

"We have to work on strength and fine finger movement. I can help with the strength. Di will help with the fine movements. Ready for your treatment?"

Ray nodded, and Sim turned and grabbed the large box he'd set on the table when he came in.

As he set it up, Bonnie helped Ray sit forward as she removed the pillows. Sim brought the pad up and nodded for him to slide farther down in the bed. Once set up, Ray laid back on the pad.

"Close your eyes. Let us do the work," Bonnie said.

"Okay," Ray said, shutting his eyes.

They worked silently for a few moments. Like the time before, Ray could feel Sim's hands on his hands, then felt the energy flow into his body, causing his hands to twitch slightly.

"I'm going to work on his ears and eyes in a little bit." The words settled in Bonnie's mind. She nodded.

"I want you to move down here. I'm going to take your hand. I want you to switch vision and see what I do."

Her head shot up. She'd never told anyone about her vision.

"What? You think I didn't know? Bonnie, girl, I know everything." The last words took on a teasing note, even in her mind.

Aloud, she said, "Ray, I'm going to move down to your wrist and hand. I want to feel your pulse. Is that okay?"

He nodded, his eyes still closed.

She moved down the bed, her hand trailing down his arm. With the other hand, she reached out and laid her hand on top of Sim's. With a slow blink her vision changed, and she saw what Sim did. She'd never seen anything like it. She could see within Ray's body. Her hand tightened on Ray's wrist.

Ray's eyes fluttered, and he could see them through the slight opening of his lids, with them unaware. He forced his eyes not to open any wider. He swallowed. Both Sim's and Bonnie's eyes had taken on a swirling appearance as they looked at his body.

"Relax, Ray. Your pulse kicked up. Is Sim hurting you?" Bonnie asked.

Ray closed his eyes tighter, hoping he hadn't been caught. "No," he lied. "You tickled me when you moved."

"Oh. Sorry." She tightened her grip and blinked, returning her vision to normal.

"It's okay," Ray said, chuckling.

"Did you see any vagueness anywhere around his neck or head?"

She jumped as the mental words hit her brain immediately following Ray's vocalization.

"You okay?" Sim's words in her mind showed concern.

She answered Sim's question with, "*I think I like cooking better.*"

She felt Sim's laughter and reminded herself to ask him more when they were somewhere else.

"*The voice you hear in your mind is from you, not me. And, yes, I can mentally laugh, get pissed, and sob. I just use your mind to portray it.*"

"*Damn. Remind me not to think anything at all while you're in my head,*" Bonnie shot back mentally, startled that he'd read her private thought.

"*I try not to invade. Tell him I'm going to move up to his shoulders.*" He put the thoughts in while he removed his hands and signed to her. For Ray's benefit of seeing finger movement, he signed *Blah, blah, blah.*

Bonnie laughed. Ray stared at her. "Sorry," she said. "I was thinking of something else. Sim is going to move to your shoulder and let the energy flow. If it feels too strong, you must let us know. Now, close your eyes and try to relax."

After they finished, Bonnie promised to return with some coffee and a bear claw that Ray had shown a great fondness for.

As Sim and Bonnie walked down the hall, she put a thought out. "*Is it possible to injure him with what we are doing?*"

Sim signed, *Switch to signing. Not many know I can do the mental communication thing.*

Bonnie nodded and signed the question.

Sim shook his head and signed. *I can monitor his blood and energy flow to specific areas of his body. His optic nerve looks good. I'm just adding a bit of healing energy to the eyes, themselves. As to the hearing, I believe hyperacusis is more neurological than aural. We'll see if neural stimulation helps.*

Bonnie laughed, signing, *All of that was way over my head. I'm heading to the kitchen.*

The front door opened and Di and KC walked in. "Hey, guys. You all done? Think he's up for a visit."

"Wait a second and I'll let you take him a snack tray, with coffee and a bear claw."

"I hooked him, huh?" Di asked, laughing and, reaching Sim, turned up her face for a kiss.

"I don't know anyone who isn't hooked on those," Bonnie said. "Be right back."

Who's minding the store? Sim signed.

"Jasmine," Di said. "And, now, you." She turned around as Bonnie appeared with the tray. To Bonnie, she said, "You sure you don't want to take it back."

"Definitely. I think Ray has seen enough of me today. Plus, I need a kitchen break."

Di took the tray and, laughing, walked down the hallway, KC following.

She knocked on the door, calling out. "You decent?"

Thinking it was Bonnie, Ray responded, "Only if you've brought the bear claw."

Di walked in. "You better be. I brought the requisite bear claw and a visitor."

His mouth dropped open as he saw KC step into the room. "You're…you're," he stammered.

"Katerie Davis," she said and held out her hand. "You can call me Kat or KC. I'll answer to either. I'm a fan of your art."

He took her hand in his and was surprised at how such a small hand created such amazing clay sculptures. "I'll stick with KC since that's been in my mind forever. I have a couple of your pieces and absolutely love your art."

"Thank you. I have a present for you. I did it years ago after attending one of your exhibitions." She handed him a bag.

He sat up straighter and pulled a box from the bag. Pulling off the lid, he folded back the tissue paper. Nestled softly within its folds was a small sculpture of an artist standing in front of an easel, his back to the viewer. The only color came from the canvas on the easel, bits of the color showing from the sides of the artist, his arm up as if he was about to add more to the canvas. Ray stared at it, turned it, and saw his profile in the artist. "Oh," he said. "It's me. That one of my first, Light Eternal."

"I know I didn't do it justice. But I wanted to capture something of what I felt when I saw you working. I had stopped by to introduce myself, but you were so enraptured that I just stood there and watched. I created this but never got to give it to you. I heard you'd been ill. Then you just disappeared. I'm so glad I can personally deliver it to you."

"I don't know what to say." He held it in his hands and felt emotion flooding him. He looked up. "Thank you doesn't begin to express my feelings."

KC looked at Di, who nodded. "I will take the thank you, but I have a favor to ask. Di and I have worked together a few times to help others with some physical injuries. We'd like to work with you to reclaim your strength and fine finger movement. Sim will work on some strength and Di with fine dexterity. I would like to work with you using clay. It would definitely involve all of the above."

"You?" he asked, then realized he was babbling. "Let me put my brain back in my skull and start again."

KC laughed.

"I would be honored to work with you both," Ray said.

"Trust me, it would be our pleasure. We are both fans."

Di, who'd set the tray on the table by the window, pulled out a couple of paperbacks from a bag. "Look what I found at Chapters." She handed him the books, taking the sculpture. "I'll put this on the table for you. By the way, I want those books back. I haven't read them," she added.

"You know, I've never actually seen them in print form. I have the digitals. They look pretty good," he said and handed them back in exchange for the tray she held out.

"Not a bad exchange. Books for bear claws," he said and took a bite of the pastry.

Chapter Nine

Ray stood at the window, watching the rain fall. He'd been hearing people arrive all afternoon and knew Bonnie would be coming for him soon. Funny how he come to prefer his solitude. Maybe it wasn't a preference, more of an acknowledgment that, in his past life, as he'd come to think of it, he'd been wearing more of his public persona than he'd have liked.

In the last week, he'd had treatments three times a day, exercises twice a day, drawn for hours, and sculpted just a few less. He'd come to the conclusion that, although his hands were definitely stronger, sculpting would never be his medium.

Yet, he'd loved working one-on-one with KC. He'd watched her work clay from a lump into an exquisite form in no time. Try as he might, his efforts went from lump to smooth or indented lump. Yet, they had become friends in that time.

He'd had better luck with Di's therapy. Or, maybe it was a combination of the strength KC had helped him gain and the dexterity that was returning to his fingers. No matter what the cause, he was enjoying sketching again.

Movement in the back, near the willow, caught his attention. He waited, but no one appeared. He squinted. Nothing. He blinked. Suddenly, the world shown in a myriad of colors. Within those colors, he saw a shifting outline. Movement. He blinked again. The world returned to normal.

He blinked once more. The colors reappeared but there was no movement.

At the sound of the knock on his door, he closed and rubbed his eyes. This was not what he'd experienced before and it made him feel a bit queasy. He grabbed a glass on the table and took a sip of water.

"Come in."

Bonnie opened the door, smiling. Seeing him, her smile faded. "Ray, are you okay?" She walked over to him, putting her hand on his arm. She adjusted his pulse and blood pressure.

Ignoring the furrows on his forehead, she looked him in the eye. "I haven't seen a spike like that in a week. What happened?"

"I think I have a bit of nerves. I haven't been with this many people in a long time," he lied. He watched her visibly relax.

"Just think of them as a lot of extended relatives you don't see but every five years or so. You only have to deal with them at dinner and then they will all go home."

"Thanks. When you put it like that…. Besides, with you by my side—you will be by my side?"

She slipped her arm through his. "Absolutely. We always bring in people to serve. We've been cooking all day and now we feast." She led him to the door and adjusted his pulse one more time. "Relax. We've got this." With that, she led him to the dining room.

They stepped into a rearranged dining room. The tables had been pulled together in a large U-shape. A long buffet was set up along the side kitchen wall. People got up, moved along the buffet, and headed back to the large table, nodding and smiling at Ray as they passed.

Teresa came out of the kitchen and saw Ray. She walked over and gave him a hug, turning back to the room. "For those of you who haven't had a chance to meet our guest, this is Ray Grissom." For those that hadn't already heard, the word "guest" told them what they needed to know. He was an outsider.

People nodded and said welcome as Teresa led him to the nearest table, where she sat him next to Bonnie. Surrounded by her and Mike, Dorian and Morgan, Morgan's adoptive parents, Jasmine and Eryk, as well as Ozzy and Sandra, he was encircled by the top descendants and safe from any slip-ups.

Ray noticed that, at the top of the tables, Sim sat with Di next to the sisters, Alice and Grace. He looked down one side and recognized Brenda from the Post Office and Jenn and John. KC sat next to a man he hadn't met. He assumed it was Rowe, her husband, who was John's brother. Claire was sitting farther down the table, holding court. Ray had come to realize that the two sisters were as different as night and day. Ray definitely preferred the quiet, sultry one.

He looked over at Bonnie, who was sipping sweet tea and nodding to Teresa. Bonnie put down her tea and stood. "Let's go get a plate," she said to Ray. "You haven't tasted Thanksgiving until you've tasted ours."

Ray loved being with her. With her in her element, it was an unexpected treat. She was vibrant and more open than he'd seen her before. What he didn't know was that Bonnie's confidence came from being with and helping him.

Ray thought as he heaped food on his plate, Bonnie couldn't have been more right. With Ray's parents being dedicated professors, holidays at home were minimal. Thanksgiving was always at someplace other than home. Some years, it was at a fancy Washington restaurant, others at another professor's house. One year it had been at one of the many embassies along Embassy Row. No matter where, it was always subdued. Of course, once he left home, Thanksgiving had been pretty much skipped. To share all this food with so many people who treated each other as family, teasing, laughing, and wisecracking was an eye-opener. It was loud and fun. And, he'd been included like he'd always been a part of that family.

One thing he immediately noticed was that the children were not set apart at "children's tables" but sat with their families and were included in the discussions. Aby sat between Teresa and Mike and Morgan and Dorian's twins between them.

With Sandra's pregnancy in full bloom, she was teased unmercifully about the newest descendant due around Valentine's Day.

Several times during the meal, either Sandra or Bonnie jumped up to issue instructions to the caterers, but Teresa was adamant in that they were not working. At one point, both women turned and glared at Teresa, making her bust out laughing.

As the evening wore on, Bonnie had mellowed, and after a couple of glasses of wine and a small amount of coaxing, she agreed to sing a duet with her sister, Claire.

The twins rose and met at the head of the tables. Each one drew one of the old sisters up, standing on either side of the older women, their arms linked. With a bit of brogue thrown in, Bonnie started singing "Loch Lomond". Claire joined in, followed by the sisters, their voices forming a harmony that sent chills up Ray's arms. At the end, the entire room was filled with song, voices joining one by one, including Ray. He watched the girls hug each other and the older sisters and would swear he'd never seen such love. Tears glistened in Bonnie's eyes as she returned to the table.

"You okay?" he asked as she sat down and took a sip of wine.

"Oh, yeah. We've actually been doing this since we could stand. The sisters would babysit us, and they taught us the song. With some encouragement and a bit of wine, we do it every Thanksgiving. And every Thanksgiving, I cry."

She stood and held out her hand. "Let's take a walk. This will be the last time you'll see the fall decorations. Tomorrow, they come down and Christmas takes its place."

He took her hand and followed her into the night filled with the lights and scents of fall.

Chapter Ten

The rain had ended, leaving a glistening sparkle on all the fall foliage. A warm evening for November, they moved down the stone steps, still holding hands. Being Thanksgiving, all the shops were closed but had left the window displays and outside lights on. Lamppost lights reflected in the wet sidewalk, spreading a magical glow. The large tree in the median glistened in fall orange and blended with the fall colors illuminated in the spraying water of the fountain.

Ray had walked Main Street a couple of times since he started feeling better, but never at night, and it mesmerized him. He'd seen some of the best and this topped even that. He turned to Bonnie. "You all do this every year?"

"Every holiday. Let's see, Thanksgiving, Christmas, we kinda skip New Year's, then we do Mardi Gras—the sisters went to New Orleans one year and decided we had to celebrate Mardi Gras. Then, there's Valentine's Day, the Spring Fling, which sort of doubles with Easter. Summer, which gets enhanced with the 4th of July, which leads us to fall. This year, we tried something new, emphasizing early fall with Halloween, then changing it to this after Halloween." She looked over at him. "What do you think? Should it stay that way or be fall longer?"

"I think you all had already taken down most of the early Halloween when I arrived, because all I remember is being blown away by this. I love this. I've never seen anything like it."

Bonnie stopped, pulling him back a couple of steps. Her smile moved to her eyes as she nodded toward the front window of Chapters, the bookstore. "When Di went to get the books to show you the covers, she told Brie about you staying at the Bed & Breakfast. Brie did some research and discovered what books had your artwork."

In the front window, situated at different heights, were five books he'd done covers for, three for Gillian, a mystery for Doylan Williams, and a science fiction for Vilma Plathman. A sign indicated that the cover art was done by Ray Grissom, a friend of Ruthorford.

"Throughout the year, the Bed & Breakfast hosts quite a few writers' groups. Can't hurt to have some advertising," Bonnie said, tilting her head to watch him.

"I'll have to stop by and thank them. That was really nice."

They started walking again.

"Those groups bring lots of business to our little town."

"Have you always stayed here? Ever gone out in the big ole world?"

"I went off to college for a couple of years. Then, mom got ill. Claire had gone to New York to learn the fashion industry and marketing. She really loved it, so I came home to take care of mom. Sandra offered me an apprenticeship at the Bed & Breakfast, and I think I found my calling."

"Is your mother better?" He had noticed a sadness in her eyes.

She shook her head. "Not really. She suffers from fibromyalgia. It can get severely debilitating. Claire lives with her now. I have the apartment over Fashion Flare. When Claire goes on buying trips, I stay with mom."

"What did you study in college?"

They had stopped in front of Elements. He looked at the window display. "I love that tooled computer case," he said, nodding at a display, then looking back up to see the store's name.

"Dink will be open this weekend. Tomorrow is the decorating blitz, so the stores are closed. Saturday will be business as usual. Everything in Elements is of Native origin."

His brow furrowed.

"Okay, Ruthorford 101. Most of the residents in Ruthorford are either of Scot descent or Native American or offspring of them. Everything in Elements is from our local Native Americans."

"I'll have to come visit. I see a few things I really like."

"I see Christmas shopping in your future." Bonnie laughed as she led him across the street. "Speaking of which, I have a terrific scarf for Gillian. You mentioned you wanted to get her a present." Bonnie put a code in the keypad at Fashion Flare and opened the door. She hit the lights and moved to the counter. Where the scarf had been neatly folded, a note was tented. "I took it up to your apartment. You keep forgetting it. C"

"Come on," she said, leading him through the back and turning off the lights as she pulled the door open. He followed her outside and waited for her to put the code in.

"Upstairs," she said and led him up some wide wooden stairs. As they reached the porch on the second floor, a loud screech sounded.

Ray's hands covered his ears.

"You all right?"

"Damn, that was loud. What was it?"

"An owl. Probably Sim's. You have your earplugs in?"

He nodded, wincing when he heard it again.

"Let's get you inside." She opened the door and pulled him inside, leading him to the living room. "Sit," she said, tightening her hand on his arm, slowing his pulse and blood pressure."

He turned, ignored the couch, and grabbed her hand. "Don't."

"I just want to help." She apologized and looked down, stepping back.

He stepped forward and put his fingers under her chin, lifting her head until her eyes met his. "What you felt had nothing to do with the owl," he said, looking into her eyes. "It had a lot to do with you."

"Oh," she said. When realization hit, she repeated, "Ohhh."

He chuckled. "Bonnie, girl, there are times you might not want to lower my heart rate." He watched the flush move up her neck to her cheeks. "Like now," he said softly and lowered his head to capture her lips with his.

Her lips were soft under his, full and warm. He let his hand move around her neck under that glorious mass of hair. Her scent of citrus and lavender, which he grown familiar with and welcomed, surrounded him. Using his hand on her neck, he pulled her closer, and she came willingly.

Bonnie had thought about this, dreamed about this, and forced it out of her mind. Now, as his mouth moved over hers, she inhaled, afraid she was forgetting to breathe, as his lips worked magic. She felt his tongue on the crease of her lips and welcomed him, easing her arms around his waist under his jacket. She could feel his muscles quiver under her fingers, and she let the kiss go deeper.

A soft warmth surrounded them and Bonnie felt a hum deep in her being. The warmth became hotter, as did the desire, until she ached.

Ray slowly broke the kiss and leaned his head against hers. "God, girl. You are pure magic."

She stepped away from him. "The scarf," she said, and her voice came out with a sultry note, causing him to look up and lock eyes with her.

"Yeah, the scarf," he said. That wasn't what he was thinking about. Feeling her under his hands seemed to take over his mind. His heart hammered and desire soared. He'd never reacted to a woman so fast and so completely as he had this woman.

She turned, walked over to the table, saw it folded there, and carried it back to him, feeling his eyes riveted on her. "I think she'll like this," she said, handing it to him.

"Um-hm," he said, taking the scarf and not looking at it. He gave his head a tiny shake. "I better go, or I'm going to do my best to make you ask me to stay."

"Well, then we both better go. I want to see if I can do anything to help them clean up."

They were almost to the Bed & Breakfast when he stopped her. "You never did tell me what you studied in college."

"Neurophysiology," she said in passing and started up the stairs.

"Seriously?" he asked, following her. "I would have thought fine arts or culinary arts, given your amazing gift with food. Not neurophysiology. Why?"

At the porch, she stopped and turned, laughing at him. "Because I'm a science geek. Just think about how much science actually goes into cooking. Plus, with mom ill, I don't see going back any time soon. I love cooking. It's not a bad compromise." With that, she opened the door and walked into the lobby. Most had cleared out of the dining room. A few stragglers remained, discussing the decorating to follow the next day.

Ray touched Bonnie's arm. "I'm going to go put this away and then come back. I can help if you like."

"You don't have to."

"No, but I would love to have some coffee with you when you're done."

Her eyes twinkled. "Want to check my science acumen?"

"Heavens, no. I wouldn't know where to begin. I'm a total art major. Dropped chemistry three times. But, I'd listen to you talk all night, even if it is over my head."

"I would love to have coffee with you. I'm sure we can find mutual ground. Why don't you come back in an hour? I bet I might even come up with another piece of pumpkin pie."

He watched as she walked away, stopping to hug the sisters on the way to the kitchen. Turning, he walked down the hall to his room. Heavens, that girl packed a punch in a single kiss.

He took the time to call his mom and dad and wish them a Happy Thanksgiving. As predicted, they'd gone to Bourbon Steak in Georgetown for dinner, which meant there would be none of the aromas there that still filled the air here. Or the loose camaraderie. Looked like this place had spoiled him in one meal.

In an hour, he moved back down the quiet hallway. No one was around. As he stepped into the dining room, Bonnie stepped out of the kitchen, her purse over her shoulder.

"I'm sorry. I need to go take care…help care for mom."

"Oh, Bonnie, I'm sorry. Anything I can do?"

She stood on tiptoe and kissed his lips softly. "No, but thank you. Raincheck?" she asked, looking toward the lobby.

He turned. No one was there. "Where's everyone?"

"Upstairs. Teresa will be down in a bit to lock up. Why don't you call it an early night? We might need to put you to work tomorrow."

He walked with her to the door. "I'd love to help tomorrow," he said and, reaching up, softly stroked at the frown lines on her brow. "Don't worry. She'll be okay."

"Thanks. I'll see you tomorrow."

Ray watched as she stepped outside and stood for a moment, looking up and down the street before quickly making her way toward her apartment. He stood there until he saw her car pull out onto the side street and turn left onto Main. As he watched, he thought he saw movement to his right, at the alley. He stepped out onto the porch but saw nothing. Suddenly, he felt a tingle, like he's walked over carpet and something had touched his thigh. He shivered, turned, and went back inside, pulling the door closed behind him. As he made his way down the hall, he heard the screech of an owl.

Bonnie, keeping an eye on the rear-view mirror, drove slowly down Main, barely coasting, until she saw Ray disappear inside. At the last moment, she swung down the alley toward the field behind the shops. She turned right again and drove past the back of the shops, stopping at the alley across from the Bed & Breakfast. Turning, she slipped past the big Victorian and pulled into the parking lot between the Chapel and the small cemetery next to it.

Bonnie walked down the narrow lane behind the chapel and crossed over to the Bed & Breakfast, slipping her card into the lock. Remembering Ray's sensitive hearing, she tiptoed to the small service elevator in the back, got inside and hit 4, barely breathing until she got out in a storage room in Teresa and Mike's penthouse. She looked in the library and, finding it empty, turned toward Aby's room.

Teresa stood looking down at her daughter in her crib. She turned and smiled at Bonnie. "Thank you for coming. I apologize for all the subterfuge." She led the young woman to the library.

Bonnie reached out and put her hand on Teresa's arm. "You know it's my pleasure. Do you want to go down to The Shoppe of Spells?"

Teresa looked toward the hallway and her daughter's room.

As if reading Teresa's mind, Bonnie spoke. "Go. Mike's at the clinic. Claire's got mom. I've got Aby. I heard another owl as I was driving down Main. See if you can do anything to help Morgan and Dorian."

Teresa nodded and headed toward the elevator when Bonnie grabbed her arm. "Go out the back," she whispered. "I told Ray you'd be down to lock up later. Make noise when you come back in."

Teresa nodded and stepped into the storage room, looking back.

"Aby will be fine. If anything happens, I can handle it."

Teresa used her key to unlock the door at The Shoppe of Spells. Jasmine was in the kitchen and looked up as she entered. "The twins are asleep upstairs. Sim says he identified five owls. He's trained them so only Oho sounds the alarm. How he did that still amazes me," she said.

Teresa looked toward the back door. "Anything yet?"

Jasmine shook her head, "Nothing that I know of. Sit down. I'll get you some decaf." She had no sooner set the mug in front of Teresa than they heard a commotion in the back. Di walked in, followed by John.

"Morgan and Dorian are staying in the cottage in case they can get it to come back. It wanted to go through but couldn't," John said and headed toward the front door.

"Sim went around one side, Eryk around the other. Damned thing got away," Di said. "Morgan and Dorian opened the portal in the cottage. This creature was too damned big. I've never seen anything like it. Of course, I've never seen it, anyway, until tonight, holding Sim's hand. Just drawings. Sim said it was over twice the size of the Gulatega he's seen before. I'll tell you what. Every hair on my body stood on end."

Teresa walked over and took Di in her arms. "Why were you even in the cottage?"

"I wanted to see it. I was with Sim. I knew I was fine."

"But those things could affect you." Teresa stepped back, studying her daughter. "Any headache, confusion?"

"Mom, you're holding onto me. You know what I saw and that I'm okay."

"You're right," Teresa said. She stopped, thoughts racing through her mind. "Ray...." her voice trailed off. She looked back at Di.

"What about Ray?" Di asked.

"The things he was experiencing when he came," Teresa said, remembering his symptoms. "Do you think he could have come in contact with the Gulatega?"

"Mom, he had the symptoms before he came to Ruthorford. Plus, he had a clot."

Teresa ran her hands up and down Di's arms. "I know. Don't mind me. It's been so long since we've had a sighting. It just puts me on edge. I don't know how it could affect Aby. After all, she's part non-descendant."

"And she's here, with all of the descendants having her back. She's fine."

They sat down and Jasmine served up coffee. It wasn't long before Sim and Eryk came in the front door, Dorian and Morgan coming in from the back.

"We opened that portal several more times. The portal is dead." Dorian said.

Sim started signing. *It just disappeared. I saw its energy go around the side of the building. I was right behind it. By the time I got the gate open, it was gone. I scanned the entire street. Nothing. Once it's far enough away, we can't see it.*

Morgan sank down into a chair. "It was so much bigger than the others. We heard the owl screech and sent out the messages. Dorian and I went to the back and opened the portal. At first, there was nothing, and it closed. About ten minutes later, I felt something, so we opened it again. I saw its outline in the room, heading toward the portal, its eyes glowing. Seeing the size, we stepped back, giving it room." She shivered and made a face. "Plus, I really didn't want to be any closer to it than I had to be. It kinda slunk between us and should have gone right through. But it stopped, backing up. It moved forward again and stopped. Then it turned and fled."

***

Ray got up, the pain in his head waking him. He grabbed a bottle of water, took a Tylenol, and walked over to the large bank of windows overlooking the back. The lights on the willow were out, but the moon had peeked out from behind the clouds and shown light across the creek. Ray pinched the bridge between his nose and rubbed his eyes.

When he looked up, his vision had shifted. The night looked similar to what he'd seen when he'd had his full range of color, except now it seemed more alive. He appeared to be able to sense something else. Heat? He saw movement. It looked like the outline of a large dog. He blinked, and the scene reverted back to normal. No animal. He blinked again and saw the movement once more. The animal stopped, turned toward him, and stood on its hind legs, its eyes glowing. He stepped back and tripped over the chair. Pulling himself up, he looked outside, but his vision had returned to normal. He blinked. There was no animal.

His head was pounding. He stumbled into the bathroom and turned on the water, splashing his face. Grabbing the towel on the side of the counter, he rubbed his face and looked in the mirror. His eyes glowed. "What the hell?" he asked out loud, reached over and flipped the light switch. His eyes had a swirling appearance. He blinked, and when he opened his lids, he saw the normal gold they had always been.

Ray whirled around and threw up in the toilet.

Chapter Eleven

No matter how tired he was from lack of sleep, his hearing, even with the high-quality earplugs, wasn't letting him sleep through the racket in the lobby and dining room. Checking in the mirror to make sure his eyes weren't swirling—and they hadn't since about two in the morning— he threw on a pair of jeans and a sweater and headed toward the lobby.

"There you are," Teresa said, a large basket in her arms.

Ray rushed over to take it from her.

"Perfect," she said, her eyes twinkling. "You can put these on each door down the hallways. Adhesive hangers are in the basket."

He turned and looked down the hall, momentarily confused. Then, he remembered what Bonnie had said.

"Here," Teresa said, leading him to the counter. "First, put that over here and go get some coffee and a pastry. Then get to work. You have three floors to do, then you can help with the porch while I decorate the tree."

He looked around. There was no tree in the lobby. She just patted his arm and rushed off.

Ray set the basket aside and walked into the dining room as Bonnie came out of the kitchen carrying a tray of mugs. He took the tray and held it while she unloaded the mugs. "I hear there's coffee and pastries."

"Ahhh," she laughed. "I see Teresa's already cornered you." She flashed him a smile that warmed his insides as she nodded to the end of the table. There's the B & B's great coffee, cream, creamer, sugar, and sweetener. Pastries under the glass covers. "Use paper plates, since we're feeding everyone today. Enjoy!" She stood on tiptoe and kissed his cheek, grabbed the tray, and rushed off to the kitchen, talking to Sandra before the door was fully closed.

He fixed some black coffee, picked up a cheese Danish, and walked over to the bank of windows. The sun streamed across the back, glistening on the water of the creek. A light breeze ruffled the feathery branches of the willow. This was a far cry from what he'd seen last night. As much as he wanted to, he refused to blink. He'd learned last night, after hours of practice, that he needed to force the vision change by closing his eyes and putting something like pressure from his brain to his eyes. He'd finally been able to do it at will. It wasn't exactly like what he'd had before, but close. He had the magnitude of colors—hell, maybe more—but he also had this outline thing. He wasn't sure what that was. And, he didn't have it all the time, either the colors or the outlines.

At first, he was pissed. He'd seen Bonnie's and Sim's eyes both change. Had they done this to him? Then he thought of Covid. He knew that tetra-thing was rare. Maybe only people with the tetra-thing had that swirling appearance. Honestly, he'd never paid attention to his own eyes. Why? Because they seemed normal. Maybe the swirling was his mind seeing the eyes through the tetra-thing. Hell, he didn't know. He took a drink of coffee and a bite of pastry and closed his eyes as the perfect flaky sweetness filled his mouth.

"I have the same reaction," Teresa said beside him.

He swung around, startled that he hadn't heard her. She grabbed his arm, steadying him to keep the coffee from sloshing.

"I didn't hear you."

"The power of the pastry," she chuckled. Her smile faltered, then came back. "I didn't mean to startle you. I just wanted to tell you Sim said if you need a treatment, he can try for tomorrow. He's kind of busy today."

Ray shook his head. "I'm good. Monday or Tuesday, or whenever he's free will be fine."

"Good. I'll let him know. In the meantime, I've set baskets of wreaths around. If it's a door, it gets a wreath. Gotta run." And she was gone.

He popped the last of the pastry in his mouth and washed it down with the rest of the coffee. There was a big basket of wreaths on the table. He looked around. Door to the kitchen and French doors. There were a lot more wreaths than for just those doors.

"One on each window," Bonnie said as she walked over and took his mug.

"I've never—"

"Just make it so guests can see out when seated at the tables. The rest is up to you. And…have fun!" She patted his arm and rushed back to the kitchen.

With a bit of trial and error, he finally got the hang of the hangers. His artist's eye came in handy for positioning, enabling him to keep them even. Fortunately, all the wreaths were the same. That made it a lot less complicated.

Ray looked down the long hallway and admired his work. He figured he'd earned another cup of coffee and hoped there might be another pastry left since it was almost lunch. He never realized how many doors there were in this place. By the time he finished the third floor, he was glad the fourth floor belonged to Mike and Teresa. He grabbed the basket and headed down on the elevator.

When he stepped off of the elevator, he stopped, stunned. In front of him was a tree in front of the lobby windows that stood a good fifteen feet tall or higher. He set the basket on the counter and walked over. Teresa was perched atop the tallest stepladder he'd ever seen.

She looked down at him. "Doors done?"

"Yes, ma'am. Can I help here?"

"Nope. We've got this. You get something to eat, and then, since you are so good at the wreath thing, I'm going to let you hang all the wreaths on the outside windows along the porch. They are bigger. And the swags for the lights and the garland for the porch rails are also out there. There's a picture on the counter." She pointed to the lobby counter. "You can use it as a guide. If you like something else, do it."

"Yes, ma'am," he said and headed to the dining room, his stomach rumbling.

"There are some sandwiches on the buffet. Put some protein in that stomach," she ordered.

"Yes, ma'am," he replied.

"Dinner is on us tonight. Kinda late, but filling."

"Something to look forward to," he called back.

Teresa watched him as he filled a plate at the buffet and grabbed a seat by one of the windows. She'd taken a moment to run over to The Shoppe of Spells while he was upstairs taking care of the doors. She wanted them to know what she'd "seen" when she'd touched him. Apparently, he'd spotted the creature before it made its way to the cottage, then again when it ran off, down by the creek. It hadn't been spotted since by anyone else. And, the owls had gone quiet. That was the good news, maybe. At least it gave them a moment to get the decorations up. Then, they needed to get back on its trail because it wasn't safe for any human with a Gulatega loose, at least anyone who wasn't a descendant.

The other thing she wanted was to make sure they knew about what he'd experienced with his vision. She was confident that Morgan and Dorian would make sure Sim knew. She'd tell Bonnie later. She sure as hell didn't want Bonnie or Sim being confronted by Ray unprepared. His emotions were bubbling underneath like a simmering volcano. She'd felt them.

Ray finished up his ham and cheese sandwich, potato salad, and sweet tea and headed out, stopping to study the picture on the counter in the lobby of how the bed & breakfast looked decorated. There were a lot of decorations on the front, from the light posts at the street and parking area, the full porch, to the upper windows.

"Don't worry about the upper windows. Eryk will come by later. You just take care of the porch."

He nodded. "Is everything out there or do I need to go get something?"

"Everything you need is on the porch."

"Okay." He turned and walked across the lobby to the front doors.

"And, Ray," Teresa started, stopping him.

"Yes, ma'am."

"Thank you. We really appreciate your help."

"It's my pleasure. Never did much decorating."

She stopped hanging the ornament in her hand, turned, and looked at him.

He just shrugged. "Not a big priority for our family."

She laughed. "Well, I can assure you, you'll get your fill today."

"Kinda fun," he smiled at her and walked outside. Stopping on the porch, he looked down Main Street. People were everywhere, carrying wreaths, stringing lights, and hanging garland. He could hear the laughter and merriment as people handed off decorations, one to another. Even Miss Brenda, the Post Mistress, was outside, a wreath in her hand.

As she started to climb a rickety ladder, he hopped down the steps and ran across the street. "Let me do that for you. Just tell me where you want it."

She stepped off the ladder and handed him the wreath. "I'm afraid I might be getting almost as old as my ladder. Thank you. Just hang it up there, under the eave, over those doors. There should be a nail already up there."

He climbed up and, leaning over, placed the wreath. "Straight?" he asked.

She stepped back and studied it. "Perfect."

"Anything else?"

"No. I keep it simple."

He smiled, looking at the garland outlining all the windows and the swags under the side lights. He pulled the ladder together. "Where do you want this?"

"Oh, just lean it beside the door. John will be by to pick it up later."

"You call me if you need anything else. I'll be over there working on the porch." He set the ladder against the wall.

He turned as she tugged on his arm, pulling him downward. She reached up and lightly kissed his cheek. "You sure are a nice guest to have around. We thank you."

He jogged back over to the porch and looked at the boxes. Laying out the garland across the rocking chairs, where they would swag under the rails, he saw the clips anchored in the wood. After a couple of hours, he had the garland hung and the wreaths on all the windows. As he moved around the side of the porch to hang another wreath, he noticed a pile of greenery. He walked over and picked it up. There were boughs of fresh mistletoe, bright white berries on some and red on others. He didn't remember it on the picture, but he grabbed one and hung it where the garland attached at each post. It looked great, so after he'd hung the wreaths, he put up the rest of the mistletoe and found he was short one.

Walking back to the door to ask Teresa where to find it, he heard a flap of wings and stepped over to see a huge white owl fly to the rail on the side of the porch with a bough of mistletoe in its beak. Stretching its wings, it landed on the rail and dropped the bough on the porch. It turned its head, looked at Ray, and made a rather guttural sound before hopping around, flapping its wings, and taking off.

"That's Oho," Teresa said behind him.

He jumped. He'd been so absorbed in the owl that he didn't hear her. That was twice now. Given his hearing, that really surprised him. "That's one large bird."

"He's as gentle as they come. He befriended Sim when they were both younger. When I was young, one befriended me. I miss him."

"I've never seen one."

"This is a bit south for them, but they decided they like it here and roost some in the sisters' barn. I see he brought mistletoe."

"I hung the rest of it but was short one and there he was."

She turned and walked down the steps, turned and looked back. "Wow. Normally, we'll get one and I hang it from the light. I guess Oho has taken a liking to you. I like what you've done with it."

He attached the last mistletoe and stacked the boxes together. "If you want me to do the upper windows—"

"Oh, no. My insurance won't cover you crawling around on my roof. Besides, you've been working all day. Take a break. Because you worked so hard, I can take a break and enjoy my daughter some. Go get some pie. You've earned it."

"I think I'll get some pie and take it to my room. I still have some homework I need to do for Di." In truth, he wasn't quite ready to face Bonnie for any length of time. He had some thinking to do.

"Is it helping?" Teresa asked, looking at his hands.

"It is. I'm able to sketch longer and it's beginning to feel natural again. I owe her and KC. I never thought I'd be able to use my hand like that again. Di's a tough teacher. She not only pushes my dexterity, she adds comments on my work. Don't tell her, but I've learned a lot. I'm surprised she doesn't have her own assemblage. Has she ever had a showing?"

"Di says art therapy is her calling. I admit she has a natural talent. When she was young," Teresa said, deciding a little fabrication might be called for, "Di told me she was going to be an art teacher. Then, one of her friends got her hand caught in a car door. Di used art to help her friend recover the use of her hand. That was, as they say, all she wrote." She made a mental note to relay that story to Di, in case he asked. "On that note, you better go do your homework." Teresa laughed and pushed him toward the door.

"Did you want me to put those boxes somewhere?"

"No. John will collect them all later." She watched him head into the dining room and was relieved at the change in his energy. Working him hard apparently let him work off some of what he had been carrying that morning.

"Do you want that heated?" Bonnie asked as she saw Ray pick up a plate with apple pie on it.

"No. I'm going to just add this whipped cream," he said, adding a large dollop on top of the pie. "I have homework to finish."

She noticed he hadn't looked her in the eyes as he had before. "Is everything okay," she said, her voice dropping a little.

Ray forced himself to look up and smile into her eyes. "I'll admit, I'm a little tired. But I really enjoyed the decorating. He picked up a mug of coffee and set the pie on top of it. "Be sure and tell the sisters I took a large piece."

"I will. Enjoy." Before he could say anything else, she turned and pushed through the kitchen door.

Teresa waited until she heard Ray close his door before walking into the kitchen. She couldn't wait any longer to talk to Bonnie.

***

Ray set the pie and coffee on the table and took a bite of pie. It was the best pie he'd ever had. The spice was a bit stronger and a little different, but he was fast becoming addicted. Good thing he had a high metabolism or he'd leave Ruthorford fat as a pig.

He took one last bite and pushed it aside, pulling his sketch pad in front of him. He wiggled his fingers, stretched his hands, picked up a pencil, and started making circles, then lines, increasing and decreasing the pressure of the strokes. He flipped a page and started again. He focused on the paper and the random marks, then started adding more. No...not quite right. He thought back, adding marks where the light had hit. There had been more definition on the side.

When he turned the page, he worked on the head and the eyes. What he'd give for his studio and paints. He blinked and looked at the paper. No matter how he moved his thoughts, he couldn't reproduce what he'd seen outside on paper. It looked like some sort of animal with cat-like eyes. Maybe lizard. No. He grabbed his eraser and tried again. And those marks on the side. They looked almost like some sort of vestige of a wing. He stared at the drawing. Lengthening the neck, he stared. Shit, he'd just drawn a young version of the dragon from a favorite childhood book, Dragon Rider.

He shoved the drawing away and pulled back the pie, scooping up the final bites, washing it down with lukewarm coffee.

Chapter Twelve

Bonnie was delegated to kitchen duty to start dinner while Sandra stayed in the lobby, keeping an eye on things. Teresa grabbed Aby and headed to The Shoppe of Spells since she was the one who knew what Ray had seen.

Mike was already in the kitchen when Teresa arrived. Seeing who all was in that common room, she turned over the sign and locked the door.

Handing off her daughter to Mike and accepting a mug of coffee from Morgan, she reported all she'd viewed when she'd touched Ray.

"I thought you said he didn't have any descendant traits," Eryk said to Mike.

"I did, and he doesn't. I rechecked with Jim," Mike said and gave Aby a noisy kiss on the cheek, making her squeal. The Abbott House in Atlanta had a state-of-the-art lab equipped with just about anything needed for studying the descendants. "Sim, I don't think you should continue with the energy therapy. Apparently, it worked too well."

Sim shook his head and signed, *I don't think it was the energy. With all the energy I've given you over the years and Di after she was shot, you two would be descendants by now. Neither of you are.*

Mike turned to Teresa. "You sure he saw the Gulatega?"

"Oh yeah. And it scared him to death. But what I was seeing through him was strange. The colors looked weird."

Sim leaned forward. *The tetrachromacy.* His fingers flew. *The energy, given for enhanced healing, may have brought back his tetrachromacy. I have no idea why it's like our viewing and not all the time, like when he arrived. The question is, what do we do. Tell him?*

Everyone looked to Jenn, sitting quietly sitting at the table, listening. "I don't think we should do anything right now. We can always tell him later. We can't take it back once we've taken that proverbial cat out of the bag." She saw them frown and continued. "I don't have a problem with outsiders knowing. Uncle Mike has known for decades. My position requires an outsider. There's Di and Ozzy. Well, Ozzy turned out to be a descendant, so he doesn't count. But you get what I'm saying. However, right now, after what happened with that militia group and the government, I'm hesitant to pull in anyone else. It's not like we are just telling him about your abilities. We are telling him about the dangers. I recommend we play it by ear. Everyone will be on their guard. We host outsiders all the time with no problem."

"Well, we don't have a Gulatega running around that they can apparently see, either," Dorian added.

"Like I said, I'd wait. But it's up to you. I can draw up an NDA and we can go that route, if you want. What happened with that creature, anyway?" Jenn gave an involuntary shudder. She'd only ever seen drawings and a possible picture of them. If non-descendants being around them could cause dementia-like symptoms, she didn't want to ever be around one. "Teresa, didn't you say he acted like he'd felt the tingle of it."

Teresa nodded. "Mike, maybe you ought to check him out."

"I will tonight."

Dorian brought the coffee pot over to the table and topped off the mugs, stopping when Teresa put her hand over her cup. "I've had too much coffee today, anyway. I need to get back since we need to get that dinner buffet set up." She stood. "Dorian, anything on the creature? I'm telling you, what he saw was a lot bigger than any I've ever heard about."

"Not a hint. It seems to have disappeared. We all know that's not the case. But the owls have gone quiet."

Teresa laughed, "Not exactly." She grinned at Sim. "I'm afraid you have some competition. Oho brought Mistletoe to Ray, with Ray standing not ten feet from him."

Sim frowned, feigned a pout, signing, *My owl.*

Teresa leaned over and kissed Sim on the top of his head. "Oho will always be your owl. However, there is something about Ray that has him intrigued. Ray handled it very well, by the way."

She took Aby from Mike, "Don't you all forget to come get something to eat. And, please, you all stay as non-descendant as possible around Ray. I've already talked to Bonnie. No blood pressure checks. Nothing. Maybe his anomalies will right themselves."

She kissed Mike and headed toward the door, turning back. "I'll wait my dinner for you, if you're not too late."

"I won't be. I want to recheck his records, then I'm heading home."

At his words, Jenn pulled out her laptop, signing in to the clinic. As the head of the Abbott Foundation, she had complete access to everything Ruthorford. Since she'd set up the VPN and firewalls, she knew she could do so securely. She swung the computer toward Mike. "Take a load off and do your magic," she grinned at her uncle.

He looked through Ray's tests and records. "I think Sim's right. It has something to do with the tetrachromacy. That clot also had an effect. Sim's energy forced some healing. It probably affected the cones, but it also may have affected his rods. Hell, I'm guessing. There's still so much we don't know about descendants. And now, we are faced with a 'normal' person," he made air quotes, "who may have enhanced abilities because of descendant ministrations. We're taking not knowing to a new level."

I'll talk to Di, not that she needs special instructions. Her art therapy is only enhanced by her talent, Sim signed.

"Oh, I definitely want her to continue. She's helped him make wonderful progress. I just want her to be aware. Besides, no one will be working with him until Monday, so he may have stabilized a bit by then. I'm going to examine him and tell him I'm cutting back the energy therapy, at least for a while—due to reports of it possibly causing neuropathy."

"Does it?" Morgan asked.

Mike made a face. "How would I know? Anything is possible."

Morgan chuckled. "That's why we love you. You make us feel so normal."

"I'll have a better answer for him. Something is niggling at my brain. He took out his phone and texted Dr. Albert, setting it on the table and picking up his mug. He was in the middle of a swallow when his phone sounded. He read the text and typed back, <Thanks.>

He stood. "I've got it. Don't worry about a thing, at least for the moment. I'm going to head over to the B & B. With any luck, I'll have dinner with my wonderful family. See you all there."

By the time Mike said hi to everyone at the Bed & Breakfast—so many had gathered to grab dinner, either to eat there or take home, it was almost eight before he could pull Teresa away. "Has Ray made an appearance?"

"No, come to think of it." She drew her brows together in concentration. "I don't think so, but I've been so busy, I honestly haven't paid much attention." She was holding a huge bowl of salad to set on the buffet and was speaking over her shoulder. "Claire is upstairs with Aby. This madhouse was even too much for her."

Mike leaned over and kissed her cheek, damp from the light perspiration curling the silver strands of hair around her face, lifting her lavender scent to surround him. He so loved that it still made him heady. Pushing down his instant desire, he focused on her flushed face. "Have you taken a break since this morning, other than at The Shoppe of Spells?"

She grinned and patted his hand. "You know how it is. I'm fine. I'm hydrating. I've snacked. I'm good. Go check on Ray."

He just shook his head and made his way through more people heading in to have some dinner, stopping to answer doctor questions. After telling about three people to come by the clinic, he finally managed to grab his doctor's bag and escape down the hallway.

"Ray," Mike called out as he knocked. After the third time, he used his master key card and eased the door open.

"Ray," he said, stepping into the room. Ray was on the bed, on top of the covers, and appeared to be asleep. Mike walked over to the side of the bed and watched the even rise and fall of his chest and the good color on his face.

He reached over and touched his arm, making sure he was far enough away that Ray didn't land a punch when he was startled. Mike had learned that one the hard way, from none other than Bill Ruthorford, Teresa's now-deceased husband, when he was ill. Mike had never been sure if that had been intentional or not, although Bill had declared apologetically that it had been an accident.

Ray's head moved from side to side, and his eyes popped open.

"You okay," Mike asked.

"What?" Ray said, frowned, and removed the earplugs.

"I said are you okay?"

Ray sat up. "What time is it?"

Mike looked at the watch on his wrist. "A little after eight."

Ray rubbed his hand over the back of his neck, moved his head, popping his neck. "Wow. I guess I worked harder than I realized."

"Can I take a look at you?"

"Say that again."

"I said, 'Can I take a look at you?'"

A smile broke out across Ray's face. "You sure can. And, for the record, it didn't sound like you were shouting at me. He looked down at the earplugs in his hand. "I guess I won't be needing these anymore." He set the earplugs on the bedside table.

Mike opened his bag and took out his blood pressure cuff. "Let's start with the basics. Your hyperacusis is gone?" he asked and inflated the cuff.

Ray nodded. "Having super hearing is not a superpower I would ever want. As well as tinnitus. Wow. I didn't realize how loud it had been."

Mike listened to the bend in his arm, watching the dial move. Smiling, he slipped off the cuff. "118/76. Pulse 65. Can't get any better than that."

"I'll have you come into the clinic for another audiology evaluation next week. I gather this is good news from the size of your smile. Mike listened to his heart and chest. "Sounds good."

He took out a penlight to look into Ray's eyes. When the light hit, Ray winced. "Light hurt?"

Squinting, Ray nodded. "A little."

"Any other symptoms?" Mike made it as casual as he could.

"I'm not sure."

"Well, pupil reflex is good. Movement is good. How about your color vision?"

"Not sure, doc." He was going to stop at that, then decided this man had saved his life. He needed to know everything. "Last night, it seemed to come back, but only when I blinked. And, when I blinked again, it turned off. I only tried it once today. Last night, when I had it on, I thought I saw something that I don't think was there. I didn't want to bother you." Color crept up his neck.

Mike knew this was his opening. "I'm not Dr. Albert, but I'm going to make a guess. It could be something called Charles Bonnet syndrome. The stroke caused you to lose part of your vision, a part you'd had all of your life. Your brain was trying to compensate for that, filling in the missing areas, possibly causing a hallucination. From what I've read, these are temporary but can take a while to resolve. As your vision corrects itself, they should decrease. Honestly, not having tetrachromacy, I can't speak authoritatively about it."

"How long?"

"Can't say. But let's not do any more energy stimulation right now. You've come so far; I'd like to see what your body is doing on its own. You okay with that?"

"Sure. What about Di?"

"Oh, I don't see any reason for you to stop the art therapy, as long as you aren't suffering tingling or numbness from it."

Ray looked down at his hands. "Not at all. I think it's helping. In fact, I'm hoping to do some of my art again." He stood and held out his hand. "Thanks, doc. I appreciate all you've done for me." Ray's stomach growled.

Mike took Ray's hand and wished he had some of Teresa's ability. "Well, let's go see what we can do about filling that void." Mike laughed, pointing to Ray's stomach. "Bonnie makes a mean spaghetti sauce. She's got meatballs on the buffet for the kids, but I always steal some. They are huge and so good. Then, there's salad to make us please the women into thinking we like healthy." He headed to the door. "Mind if I leave my bag here? I'll grab it later."

"No problem," Ray said. They stepped into the hallway. "Wow. I can smell that sauce now. I'm starving."

Chapter Thirteen

Mike and Ray entered the lobby to find Teresa talking to John and Jenn. Ray had met them both on Thanksgiving, then saw Jenn again before he started therapy. He knew Jenn was Mike's niece and John was the Native American tribal leader.

"There he is," Teresa said, walking over to Ray and kissing his cheek. "I want to thank you. Because of all the work you took on, I was able to finish the tree for the first time, just in time for dinner." She stepped back and let him see the tall tree in front of the large windows by the French doors.

The evergreen, loaded with tiny white lights, was filled with reds, golds, and silvers. Gold and silver ornaments were interspersed with boughs of red poinsettias, gold sprayed baby's breath, and white and silver iced glittering fronds. From the top, red and white glittering berry sprays fanned upward, forming a nest-like setting for a beautiful white owl. Underneath, a large red tree skirt, decorated with gold, silver, and white beaded scrolls, added to the elegance.

"That's magnificent," he said, stepping forward, studying it. His forehead creased in concentration. "I don't know why, but that seems so familiar," he said to Teresa, who'd stepped up beside him.

She looked at him, smiled, and nodded back over her shoulder. As Ray turned, his breath caught. On the wall behind the counter was one of his earlier pieces, a modern mixed media, brilliant in acrylic colors flashing out to the sides, featuring an assemblage creation with a Christmas tree in the center. He turned to Teresa. "I haven't seen this in years. I'd forgotten it. I thought it was sold to a private collector."

Jenn stepped forward. "It was. It was purchased by the Abbott House Foundation when Bill Ruthorford saw it and wanted it for our Atlanta facility. It's hung there every Christmas since. When Teresa told me who you were, I thought it would be perfect for hanging here for the season. Then, she decided to decorate her tree in honor of your art, giving it a similarity. We hope you're pleased."

"I'm stunned. It's amazing." He turned to Teresa and hugged her. "You have just given me the most incredible Christmas present."

She felt the emotion pouring off of him and sent a small amount of energy to him, calming him. "I'm so glad you like everything. Because of you I was able to take the time to do this. Why don't we go get something to eat?"

He followed her and Mike into the dining room. Except for one other table, it looked like the place had pretty much cleared out.

"You're dining with us tonight," she said and walked over to her table. As they took their seats, Sandra came through from the kitchen.

"Sweet tea for all?" she asked.

When he nodded, Teresa nodded. "Tell Bonnie to come join us. She's busted her keester in that kitchen all day, and I know she hasn't eaten enough to fill a hummingbird." She saw Ray's smile and knew she'd made a good decision. Having sensed his fear about the swirling eyes, she was concerned he would shut Bonnie out. She didn't know what Mike had said. She'd tried not to read him; but, whatever he'd said to Ray, it was to Bonnie's benefit.

Seeing the look on Ray's face change, Teresa turned. Bonnie emerged from the kitchen, her face still flushed from the heat, her sable hair full from the humidity, and her dark green eyes sparkling. With her black cable-knit sweater sleeves pushed up, she looked more comfortable and confident in her surroundings than Teresa had seen in a while.

Ray stood and pulled out the chair next to him. "I hear it's to you we owe this amazing aroma."

She stopped by the chair, smiling up at him. "Then, I suggest we fill our plates because I've been smelling it all afternoon and not eating. I'm starved."

He stepped back and let her lead the way, waiting for Teresa and Jenn to fall in behind her. As they grabbed large oval plates, Bonnie called out. "Ray, you have to try the meatballs. I got the recipe from Uncle Bill. They are to die for."

"That would be Bill Ruthorford, my first husband," Teresa said. "He passed away a bit ago. Trust me, that man could cook."

Sandra stepped out of the kitchen. "Take your plates to the table, and I'll bring a huge bowl of salad and bowls for each of you. Speaking of Bill, the salad is dressed with his famous Italian dressing, which is so good."

By the time he got to the end of the buffet, he had a plate of spaghetti with thick meat sauce and a meatball the size of his fist nestled in the middle. Waiting at the end, Bonnie lifted a ladle and spooned more sauce over the meatball. She grabbed a small plate with a cheese grater on it and headed back to the table.

"Parmesan?" she asked, then set down her plate and moved around the table, grating cheese on everyone's plate.

Sandra brought a tray with salad bowls, a large bowl of salad with tongs, and a steaming basket of garlic bread. Setting everything in seemingly predetermined spots, she stepped back. "Bon appetit!"

"Did you eat?" Teresa asked.

"Yep. I ate early, before the crowd, with Ozzy. I also sent some home with him for a midnight snack." She called back, pushing open the kitchen door with her butt.

Bonnie waited until he'd taken a bit of the meatball before asking, "And?"

"Oh my God," he mumbled, his mouth still full.

"Told ya," she said and dug into her spaghetti.

He turned and looked at her, his eyes capturing hers, her dark green eyes looking deep into his. There was no swirl. How could he have thought this gorgeous creature could be a threat. Or Sim, for that matter. Both of them had done nothing but try to help him. Mike was right. That stroke was making him hallucinate. Feeling relieved, he grabbed some Italian bread, broke it in half, and handed half to Bonnie, giving her an intimate smile.

They spent the dinner talking about the decorations and the upcoming festivities. The formal tree lighting wasn't going to happen until Sunday night, giving everyone time to put up last-minute touches. Plus, they wanted to do it early enough so all the children could participate. They'd get to do some singing, getting the season off in the right spirit.

After they were finished, Bonnie stood and started to gather plates when Teresa spoke up. "Why don't you let me help Sandra with that, and you take Ray on a tour. I think he'd like to see his handiwork with the lights on. "Ray, you might grab a coat, the temps are dipping."

"Son, would you bring my bag to me while you're at it?"

"Sure will."

"I'll meet you in the lobby," Bonnie said. "I want to check on Claire. She's babysitting."

When Bonnie stepped off the elevator, she was still flustered by the teasing her sister had heaped upon her. Ray was leaning against the counter, looking at the tree. "It's so beautiful," she said. "I think she did a good job capturing the feel of your painting."

"She absolutely did. There's a story behind that painting."

"I'd love to hear it," she said and stepped through the door he held open for her.

"My family wasn't big into Christmas. We usually spent it quietly or with others. It was at a friend's house that I first saw a Christmas tree like this. When I started my art, I guess I created that painting so I'd always have a

Christmas tree. When someone wanted to buy it, I was stunned. Ironically, the Abbott House Foundation was my first customer."

"And now you have the real thing. She did that for you, you know. She has a way of knowing what people need."

"I will never forget this place." He reached out and took her hand as they crossed the street.

"I hope not." She pulled him to a stop so he could look back. From this angle, the spotlights highlighted his work, as well as the gorgeous tree in the lobby.

"I really did that," he said almost in a whisper.

"You did great, too. I hear you have a feathered admirer."

"Yeah. Well, that scared me to death at first. I'm not sure if Teresa hadn't stepped out there, I wouldn't have run inside. I had no idea owls are so big."

"I remember when I was a little girl, I was playing in the field, sitting on the ground, making a necklace out of lavender for my mom. Out of the blue, this huge white thing swooped down, settling down next to me. It had to have been as tall as my upper body. We just sat there, staring at one another. A whistle pierced the air and the bird took off, landing on the arm of this scrawny boy, nearly knocking him over. Of course, I knew about Sim, but I didn't know him. He walked over with his owl and let me pet him. When the owl flew off, he picked up the necklace I'd been working on and took me to the sisters—they raised him—to share some pie. He helped me finish the necklace.

I had such a crush on him from that day on. The sisters are the ones that taught me sign language."

"You and Sim?"

She's stopped to look in the window of Elements. "Huh? Oh, he grew up a lot faster than I did," she defended. In reality, her insecurities had begun to take hold and she'd withdrawn from most contact, even her sister, by that time.

They crossed over to the large Victorian at the other end of town. It was all lit up, lights lining the windows and the posts on the porch. "That's Sandra and Ozzy's place. They go all out for the holidays. That little Victorian is the sisters'."

"I met them when I arrived."

"Oh, yes. They made you bring pies." She laughed. "They only do that if they like you."

He looked at her, her hand still warm in his. A breeze had picked up, moving her hair about her shoulders. He wanted to pull her to him and feel her mouth under his.

"Look," she said, breaking the moment. She pointed back toward the Bed & Breakfast.

He looked up and, from where they stood, saw the whole of Main Street in its winter finery. Even the tree, although still unlit, shown from all the lights surrounding it. He could only imagine how magnificent it would be when lit. He'd never have guessed such a transformation was possible in a single day.

"Let's head back. I want to help Sandra close up."

As they passed the shops, he waited until they got to the alley by the art gallery and pulled her to the side, merriment in his voice. "With all these Christmas lights, I can't find a dark corner to take advantage of you." He pulled her into his arms, brushing the hair from her face. "I'm going to go crazy if I don't kiss you."

Her eyes met his, then moved to his mouth.

He lowered his head and his cold lips met hers, warming from their touch. As his tongue touched the crease of her lips, she opened for him until his tongue stroked hers, causing a pull deep in her center. She knew he would leave and this would be a memory, so she fell into it, giving herself a memory worth keeping.

Feeling the magic of desire envelop them, she pulled back. "I really need to get back."

"I know. Will you come to the lighting with me?"

"I would love to," she said and placed a soft kiss on his lips.

He saw Teresa by the tree in the window, adding another ornament and loosened his hold on Bonnie, wanting more than anything at this moment to drag her up to her apartment and make love to her. He knew in his heart she wasn't one for a short affair and he would be leaving soon. Yet, he didn't want to let her go.

An owl screeched overhead as something brushed against his leg, causing a tingle to move through his body. He blinked and looked over his shoulder. "What the hell?"

Still half in his arms, Bonnie felt the energy move through her. She pulled him close with her cheek against his chest, closing her eyes. When she opened them, she saw a shape moving off toward the creek, the owl giving chase.

She hugged him closer, closed her eyes again, and listened to his heartbeat steady, which surprised her since she knew hers was going a mile a minute.

"Hey, you just shivered." She tried to sound cheerful. "I guess I kept you out too long."

"Maybe," he said. He reached up and rubbed his eyes. "I guess I'm more tired than I thought."

She could feel his pulse, it was up, yet his blood pressure was going down. Bonnie concentrated and regulated it. She didn't care what Mike had said; she didn't want him passing out on the street.

He shook his head as if coming to. "Mike said I might have some residual effects of the stroke. As much as I wanted to take you to your apartment and seduce you, I don't think that's on my agenda tonight." He laughed, trying to make light of the sudden exhaustion he was feeling.

He took her hand and walked her to the Bed & Breakfast. When they got to the steps, Bonnie put her arm through his and they walked up together, her helping him without him realizing she was doing so.

Teresa had a large mug of coffee waiting for Ray. "I thought you'd like to take this back with you." Her smile froze when she saw how pale he looked. Bonnie met her eyes, then looked toward the kitchen.

"I enjoyed the walk, but I better go help Sandra," Bonnie said, squeezing his arm. "You get some rest."

Teresa held out the mug. When he reached for it, she put her other hand over his as if to steady it. She pushed energy into him, also getting a quick view of what had transpired.

"Thanks for the coffee," he said, taking the mug and watching Bonnie disappear into the kitchen. "And I want to thank you for everything. There's so much. My life. My health. My art. You all have brought me such joy."

"And you, us," she said and nodded to his picture. "Even before we knew you."

She watched him make his way to his room before she went off in search of Bonnie, who looked as pale as he did.

Chapter Fourteen

Teresa pushed open the door to the kitchen to see Sandra watch Bonnie scrubbing down the counter for all its worth. Sandra lifted her shoulders in a shrug, grabbed the tray, and backed through the door, whispering, "She's all yours."

Hearing the comment, Bonnie swung around, sponge in hand, pointing it like a rapier. "What the hell is going on? I thought non-descendants couldn't see those creatures. Hell, I've never seen those creatures until tonight. And why did I see them, because I was being held by a non-descendant, WHO, supposedly, can't see them?" She turned back around and started scrubbing. "Regulating heartbeats and sometimes seeing auras is enough for me," she mumbled to herself. Before Teresa could say anything, she spun back, pointing again. "Why do you think I don't date? I don't want to be part of the descendancy thing. I don't want to be hooked up with a male descendant." The tears started flowing. "I thought Ray was safe. Is it me? Did I do this to him? What do I do now? He's not a descendant. This thing could really hurt him." Her words came fast, jumbling.

Teresa moved forward, took the sponge out of Bonnie's hand, laid it down, and took her into her arms. "Bonnie. I don't know what is going on. I've never seen a Gulatega like this, if it is a Gulatega. I don't know why Ray can see them. I don't know why, when you were with Ray, you could see them. But," she said, gently moving Bonnie back and brushing her tears away, "I promise you, we aren't going to let him get hurt, not if we can help it. And, caring for someone, no matter what they are, be they descendant or not, isn't always a matter of choice. You really care for him, don't you?"

Bonnie nodded and hiccupped, making Teresa force herself to not smile. Poor Bonnie's eyes had gone a brilliant green, more vivid than she'd ever seen them. Teresa grabbed a paper towel and handed it to the distraught young woman, who seemed all of fourteen at that moment and suffering through her first love.

"Why don't you get something to drink and go upstairs to the apartment. I'll be right up. Oh, and you might let your sister know you're okay, or she's going to be on the warpath, and we sure as hell don't want that."

For the first time, Bonnie grinned. "No, we don't. She could probably take down an oak with a look. I wish I had her strength." She wiped her sniffles once more.

"Bonnie, you have your own strength. You just don't recognize it for what it is. Now, go. I'll be up in a few moments."

Bonnie nodded and turned, pushing through the door. "I'm sorry," was all she said to Sandra as she rushed past her in the dining room.

"It's okay. Love you," Sandra called out, watching Bonnie flee through the lobby.

Teresa came through the kitchen doors with the cell phone to her ear, filling in Mike. "Just check on him when you get home. He should be fine until then."

She slipped the phone into her pocket as Di and Sim walked in.

"We brought some fresh pastries for the morning." Seeing Teresa's expression, Di looked at Sim, "I'll take them back."

He nodded and looked around. Eryk and Jasmine were sitting in the corner talking to Sandra. Teresa nodded toward that corner and Sim followed her over.

"I'm glad you all are here. Grab hands. I'm too tired to do this more than once."

Without a word, they joined hands. Teresa looked around and pushed the images she'd gotten from Ray tonight into all of them, adding some energy for good measure. "I don't know who of you got those images besides Sim. I need to get upstairs to Bonnie. If you didn't," she turned to Sim, "Sim will relay what happened. Mike's going to check on Ray later. I gave a push of energy to him when he came in. Bonnie is devastated. We have a real problem. I expect the descendants to help me figure it out." The last was a command, as much as anything. With that, she turned and walked to the elevator, glancing down the hall as she went.

To hell with it, Sim thought and opened his mind to the others, letting his words sink into all of their minds. "*Yes. I can do this. No time for explanations. Did you all get the images?*"

He looked around. They all nodded. None of them seemed surprised at his method of communicating. "*I will let Di know. Sandra, you relay to Ozzie. I think we need a descendant meeting at Morgan and Dorian's, sooner rather than later. But right now, I'm going to check on Oho. I am pretty certain that was my owl that chased off that creature. Tell Di to meet me at The Shoppe.*" With that, he turned and rushed out.

"Well, that was interesting," Jasmine said.

"Really. It's Sim. I wouldn't doubt anything. He's like our own superhero," Eryk toned in, shaking his head.

"What are you, chopped liver?" Jasmine asked.

"I'm not Sim," Eryk said. "Let's get over to Dorian's. Sandra?"

"I'm going to hold down the fort here, free up Teresa and Bonnie. Ozzy left to go to Virginia this afternoon after we finished decorating. Just keep us informed."

Di came out of the kitchen as they were getting ready to leave. With Di being a non-descendant, and them not being like Sim, they weren't sure what information they could pass on, so they just told her. She nodded and sent them on their way. "I'll stay and help Sandra after I go check on Ray."

Di walked down the hallway and listened at the door. She thought she heard the shower running. She opened the door and called out.

"I'm in the shower. Take a load off. I'll be out soon," came the reply.

She walked over to the table, the lamp shining down on a sketch of Bonnie. It was a gorgeous sketch, as good or better than her own work, and she knew her own worth. Curious, she flipped the pages back and stopped. There, facing her, was an image similar to what Sim had relayed to her. She flipped back a few more pages and saw different strokes and shadings and smiled. At least he'd been doing his homework. Glancing toward the bathroom, she pulled out her phone and took pictures of the sketch of the creature, turning the page back to Bonnie.

He came out in jeans and a sweater, his damp blonde hair wavy. He'd been expecting Bonnie, but the shock and disappointment showed only momentarily. "Sorry. I was so tired I thought a shower would revive me."

"And did it?" She looked at him. His color was good.

"Some," he laughed. "I guess all that work today was more than I'd expected."

Di nodded toward the sketchbook. "That's a gorgeous sketch of Bonnie."

"Thanks. I just finished it."

"Hope you don't mind, I peaked back. I see you're doing you're homework. Oh, I brought you something. She reached into her jacket pocket, pulled out a package, and handed it to him."

He took the bag and opened it, pulling out a carton. "Paint pens," he said, excited.

"I know they're only watercolor, but at least you can play with some colors now."

"Thank you. It means a lot."

"Maybe you could fill in the colors of your image here." She flipped the page to the outline of the creature.

He just shrugged.

"What is it?" She looked down and appeared to study it.

He walked over and looked. He'd avoided doing so when he got back from his walk with Bonnie, but there it was, the creature he'd seen tonight. He felt the blood drain from his head.

"Whoa," Di said. "Maybe you ought to sit down. She pulled out a chair and pulled him into it before he could respond. "You okay?"

"Yeah. Just got a little woozy." He looked up at her. "I can't fill it in. There's nothing to fill in."

She sat down in the chair next to him, studying the picture. "What exactly do you mean?"

"What the hell," he muttered, more to himself. "The other night, I was looking out the window and saw movement. When I blinked, it seemed my tetrachromacy had returned and I saw this outline," he pointed to the picture. "Except it moved. I tried to draw it and realized I'd pretty much drawn a version of a dragon from Dragon Rider." He smiled at her. "I was really into dragons as a kid." He turned the sketch more toward him and looked at it. "Mike said that after a stroke, some people get this syndrome—I can't remember the name at the moment—but it happens when there's some vision loss and the brain throws in its own version of the missing images. I figured mine threw in dragons from my childhood. Made sense. Until tonight."

"What happened tonight," she asked.

"I went for a walk with Bonnie. When we were almost here, we stopped." He hesitated, not wanting to divulge information about the kiss for some reason. "I felt a tingle, like a shock, and when I looked up there it was. Then, that huge owl chased it away. I feel bad for Bonnie. She appears to be dating, or seeing, at least, a man who's having hallucinations."

"Do me a favor, Ray. Tell Mike the next time you see him. Don't try to carry this alone. It could be that thing you said. It could be something related to Covid. We just don't know. But you are in a good place. We've got your back."

"Tell me," she continued, "when did you do that drawing of Bonnie?"

"Tonight. When I came back to the room. I just wanted something tangible to look at. Plus, I really like the way she looks." He couldn't stop the smile.

"I can tell. So, your dexterity is definitely improving. You did that fast. Take the pens and try some water coloring. Let's see how your color vision is with the tools at your disposal." She stood. "I have to run. I'm helping them close." She purposefully didn't say who.

"Thanks for stopping by," he said and walked her to the door. "Thanks for letting me get it off my chest."

"Just tell Mike about tonight," she said and headed back down the hall.

Mike was exhausted by the time he'd left the clinic. Decorating day was always a trip. He'd never known such talented people but also so many who took risks. They might have special abilities, but they were still human.

He'd set sprained ankles, doctored two goose-egg-sized lumps on heads, and given two tetanus shots—more for their stupidity than the danger of tetanus. The descendants' immune systems were off the charts. Oh, not to mention washing glitter out of eyes and setting a fracture. At least this year, neither of the sisters had taken a tumble off the porch roof.

His exam of Ray was cursory. His mental faculties seemed fine. His vitals were good. He was exhausted, but that could have been attributed to the day as much as the encounter with the creature. He'd opened up about the latest hallucination tonight, and Mike had tried to reassure him, repeating what he'd said about the syndrome. God, how he wished that was the simple answer.

Now, Claire had Aby, having sent Bonnie home, and Teresa expected him to make an appearance at the Shoppe to discuss descendant stuff. All he wanted to do was fall face-first into the bed and sleep more than five hours. But, he grabbed his bag and made his way to the shoppe, knowing his good wife would give him a "boost," helping him make it through the night.

When he opened the door to the Shoppe, there seemed to be an argument going on. He just stood there, unwilling to get into the middle. Or unable to, at this point. Teresa saw him, rose, and came over.

"Hey, handsome," she said. "Give me a kiss."

Even as tired as he was, he couldn't resist his silver-maned vixen. As his lips met hers, he felt the energy flow into him. It went straight to his gut and he felt himself harden.

"Whoa," he whispered against her mouth. "There's a lot more than an energy push in that kiss."

"You betcha. I just wanted you to feel what I feel when you take me in your arms. Plus, what better way to up your energy." She gave a throaty laugh, took his hand, and pulled him to the kitchen. "Someone get my husband a mug of coffee, please. He's dead on his feet, yet thinks enough of you all to drag his ass over here at this late hour."

Morgan handed him a steaming mug of coffee with one hand and took his other, blinked, and scanned, laughing. "Not too bad for an old man," she said when he yanked his hand back.

"Don't even," he said but felt the blush creep up his neck. "Sim, how's Oho?"

Acting like King of the roost, which he is, Sim signed. *No indication that anything is amiss. I went over and checked the barn. None of the others seemed distressed, either. I haven't seen them out swarming, like they will with the Gulatega, either. Almost like Oho has a special vendetta against this large creature.*

"Or has taken a particular liking to Ray," Jasmine teased.

"You are really pushing your luck tonight, baiting Sim," Teresa warned.

At that moment, Sim stuck his foot out and touched Jasmine's shoe, sending an energy spike right up her leg.

"Ow!" Jasmine squealed and glared at Sim.

"So, what was all the bellyaching about when I walked in?" Mike asked, hoping to diffuse the situation. It was apparent they were as tired as he was.

Dorian started. "We've opened that damned portal six times. It actually showed up twice—"

"That sucker's got a sting, too," Morgan threw in. "I'm not talking about Sim, either."

"That's why Eryk and Jasmine took it on. Eryk and I tried and kept zapping ourselves," Dorian said. "I didn't want both Morgan and me working the portal with all the unknowns. But the ying-yang thing seems to work better. "Anyway, the creature seemed to want to go through but ran away at the last minute."

"I'm telling you, that thing is too big for the hole," Jasmine slapped the table with her hand. "It won't fit."

Dorian narrowed his eyes at her, just like he'd done when they were kids and had one of their ongoing arguments. "Well, it got *in* here, didn't it?"

"Well, not *from* here, it didn't," she made a face at him.

"What about that portal in Ian's pseudo-castle in Virginia Beach?" Morgan asked, trying to bring down the energy in the room.

"You think it just traveled 600 miles?" Dorian asked.

Morgan shrugged. "Well, Ian fit through that portal, so maybe…."

Di walked into the room. "Hey, guys. I helped Sandra close up. "I have something to show you. Here, Dorian, I'll send it to you so you can put it on the computer and share it on the big screen." Which, in fact, was a shade they lowered over the window on one side of the huge round kitchen table. She waited for it to appear on the shade. "That is what Ray drew the first time he saw it."

They all looked at the screen. Sim signed, *That drawing's got more detail than what I seem to be seeing. Even more depth. It almost appears two-dimensional to me, if that's possible.*

Eryk piped up, "Me, too. It seemed almost flat. John, can you have Jenn send some of the pictures to us from the library?"

"What are you, lazy?" John asked, laughing. "We all have access to the library."

"Did they all get scanned?"

"Between Missy and Jenn, I think they did. Especially since that book came from Scotland."

"Damn, I knew I'd seen something like that before," Teresa leaned forward. "Flesh it in and you might have a juvenile version of that drawing in the back of the book."

Five voices sounded at once, "That dragon in the book?"

She nodded, pointing to the lines indicating some sort of wing-like vestige.

Jasmine scoffed, "No wonder it wouldn't fit."

Dorian glared at her.

"What?" she asked. "I was right, wasn't I?"

"Children," Teresa said, but the tone in her voice wasn't a joke. "We need to figure out just what we are going to do. And, it seems attracted to Ray. If those little things have such huge neurological effects on humans, just think what one this large would have."

Sim's fingers flew. *That may be why Oho has also taken a shine to Ray. He's protecting him. I've never seen an owl chase one.*

"Or, he's using him as bait," Eryk supplied. "Ray comes around, the creature comes around, and Oho gives chase. Maybe Oho just sees it as a giant rodent or some sort of prey."

Sim was going to chastise Eryk in defense of Oho but stopped. Maybe there was something to what he was saying.

"Jenn is talking to Meadow as we meet. Meadow's been trying to translate the symbols and language written in that text. Jenn's hoping she's made some progress."

"Wasn't Meadow going to Scotland?" Di asked.

"Covid has put that off for a while," John said. "I know she's anxious to go. Given this new development, I'm not sure how I feel about it. I don't care about all her degrees and pedigrees. I sure as hell don't want her stepping into such a dangerous situation."

Di looked at him, frowning.

"She inherited Ian's castle, keep, whatever you want to call it," John explained. "They found trunks of ancient manuscripts and drawings in the caves under it and sent them to her via the Abbott House Foundation. I'll show you pictures. With her archeology and anthropology specialties, she's been dying to get over there to do some research. I don't want her going at all right now. But, if she does, I don't want her going without someone who can help her."

The picture from the back of the book popped up on the screen. It was a drawing of a man standing next to a resting dragon, the man's hand on its neck, the dragon's wing partially around him in a protective manner.

"Holy…." Di stopped and leaned closer. "Here?"

"Don't know. Fantasy drawing is what we surmised. Not so much at this moment."

Jasmine jumped up, nearly knocking over the coffee cups. "I've got it. We've got a portal large enough."

They all looked at her. "Come on, guys. Think about it. In the descendants' cemetery."

"Yeah, and you know what has happened every time we've tried to open it. We get thrown on our asses. That seems to be beyond our abilities," Eryk said.

We haven't ALL tried, Sim signed.

"Oh, no! No, Sim," Di said, laying her hand on his arm.

He just looked at her. But his mind reached out to her, letting his love wash over her, and she felt tears gather in her eyes.

Chapter Fifteen

John sat across from Jenn in her large office at the Abbott House in downtown Atlanta. In some ways, he would always think of it as Bask's office, the CEO who'd reluctantly relinquished it to Jenn after he's been injured in an accident. But now, Bask was traveling and finally enjoying his life.

John stared at his wife. This position had a way of sucking the life out of you. She seemed to be handling it well, but he planned to keep an eye on her just the same.

"What?" she asked, glancing at him out of the corner of her eye.

"Nothing. I just love you."

"Aww," came the voice from the large monitor over on the side wall, showing Meadow grinning.

"Shuddup, *nistim*," John teased, using the Cree word for niece. "Your day will come." Since her father had died, John, although actually her cousin, had been declared her uncle, taking on a more guardian role.

"How do you know it hasn't, *nisis*?" she replied, emphasizing "uncle," as she teased him back.

"Because I'm not ready." In his mind, she'd grown up way too fast.

"Uncle, I love you. Don't worry about me. I always have my family at heart. All of my family."

He nodded, acknowledging her mention of both the Native American and the Scot lineage. As the Native leader, as well as her relative, he felt he had more to worry about. Since her recovery from the tumor as a child, she had blossomed and made both parts of her family proud. As a descendant and as a Native American, she had tackled her education with the purpose of having a firm foundation for studying both lines of her family tree. Her research in archeology and anthropology had already been groundbreaking, and she was now working with Jenn and Missy to categorize much of their recent findings.

"I wish you could be with us for the tree lighting," Jenn said.

"Me, too. I do miss you all, but Mom is so busy running Safe Harbor, I feel like I need to be here for her."

"I can't tell you how much I appreciate both her and you. Because of you two, I can be here and know Safe Harbor is there for those that need it."

"Well, if we don't get this meeting moving, we won't make the tree lighting," John interjected.

"Yes, uncle. I looked at my information and compared it to the sketch you sent. Could it be an immature or juvenile version? Possibly. But I can't say definitively. I couldn't find anything to indicate what a juvenile would look like. And, given the sketches and personal descriptions of the Gulatega, there are some similarities but also some differences. It's possible that two different animals made it through the portal."

"That is not what I wanted to hear," Jenn said, a shiver moving up her spine.

"I know. I'm sorry. I just have to look at all the possibilities. I figure all of our folklore about dragons had to come from somewhere. Why not the Gulatega?" She looked over her shoulder. "Look, I have to run. We have a late intake coming. I love you both."

"We love you, too," Jenn said. "Thank you."

"You take care. Love you," John added before Jenn signed off. He stood. "So, do we know any more than we did before?"

"Some. None of which is very reassuring," Jenn said. "Let's go light a tree and hope nothing disrupts it."

***

By the time they arrived in Ruthorford, going in the back way and parking by the office John used as a quasi-police station, they could hear the kids' laughter as several ran past the alley. They stepped out of the alley to see Ray and Bonnie coming down the steps of the Bed & Breakfast with Teresa and Mike and walked over to join them.

"How did you get Mike to step away from the clinic?"

"Threats," Teresa said simply.

"Ahh. Hi Ray. How are you?" Jenn asked.

"Good. Thanks," he said, looking down Main Street. "I had no idea there were so many people in Ruthorford." His gaze went down the center of town, filled with people milling around. The adults stood back away from the tree while the children congregated at the tree and near the old sisters. Thinking of cities in Virginia and also DC, he looked at Bonnie. "I noticed the kids aren't anywhere near their parents."

"We're a pretty tight community here. The kids are safe."

"Large, close-knit community," he said. "Not a concept I'm familiar with."

Bonnie looked up at the man she knew so little about yet cared more for than she thought possible. Teresa's talk with her had made her realize that nothing was promised and every day was precious. So, no matter how long he was going to be in Ruthorford, and no matter what they were going to face while he was, she was going to be by his side, as long as he wanted her.

Mike and Teresa moved off to talk with Jenn and John. Bonnie turned to Ray. "Up for a little history lesson?"

"Sure."

"Okay. Many years ago, immigrants came over from Scotland and made their way here. The Native Americans, who had this land, welcomed them. Then, the Scots helped keep the Natives safe when they would have been relocated. I'm sure you've heard about the Trail of Tears. Long story short, Ruthorford and the surrounding farms are a mix of Scot and Native American."

"Cool." He looked over the crowd, seeing a mix of people. "Okay, it's just that I haven't seen a lot of Native Americans running around town. At least not until tonight."

"That's because most of them own the farms surrounding the town. One of those farms raises gorgeous thoroughbred horses. Of course, one of the farms also belongs to Mike and Teresa."

"Mike's Native American?"

Bonnie stopped and looked at him, confused. "No. But the tribe allowed him to buy one." She grabbed his arm and pulled him forward. "Come on. They are getting ready to light the tree. You are in for a treat. Keep your eyes to the sky."

Ray looked at the little stand that was in front of the tree. One of the sisters crooked a finger and a little girl started to step forward, only to stop and look back, motioning. Another little girl moved up beside her. They both looked at the old sister, who smiled and nodded. Together, one redhead and one raven-haired child stepped up to the platform and, with hands joined, they pressed the button and the lights came on.

From the sky, bird calls sounded, and owls appeared from the other end of town, ribbons trailing. As the owls approached, each one released a ribbon, and it floated down, streaming down the tree. The final bird circled and perched on the top, placing a mistletoe bough in place. For a moment, the bird seemed to pose, then it took off, its enormous wings flapping.

"Pretty amazing, huh?" Bonnie asked. But Ray's eyes were riveted on the retreating owl. He watched as it flew to the end of the road and, with wide wings spread, landed on Sim's outstretched arm.

"I want to do that."

"Do what?" Bonnie asked.

Ray nodded toward the end of town at Sim. "That."

Bonnie stepped around him and looked down the sidewalk. She spotted Sim before he headed down the alley. "Sim?"

"Uh-huh. I want to handle an owl."

She looked up at him. "You sure you're okay?"

He finally looked away once Sim disappeared. "Oh, yeah. I am."

Voices in the crowd rose in song. I'm Dreaming of a White Christmas, swept through the throng of people. As if on cue, snowflakes began to filter down, swirling in a cold breeze. Kids squealed and danced in the falling snow.

Ray put his arms around Bonnie and joined the carolers, harmonizing with Bonnie's beautiful voice, pulling her back against his chest. She leaned her head back and smiled. She couldn't ask for a more perfect start to the season.

***

The next week was one Ray wanted to never end. KC had come and offered him the use of the small studio in the back of the gallery to try to expand the use of his hand so he might get back into his art. He got up early and used the natural morning light that shone through the window and skylight to blend colors on a canvas.

His sight wasn't what it had been before the stroke and Covid, but he found he could work with it. Concentrating, then closing and opening his eyes, the tetrachromacy seemed to have returned, but with a flare, literally. The colors flared out from outlines. Presently, he was trying to replicate this on canvas, using what he now called his "natural" vision to see what he figured people with normal vision would see.

Ray smiled at the canvas he'd been working on. He felt he'd been given a gift, albeit a strange one. Before, all he'd had was the tetrachromacy. Now he had both.

He looked at the clock on the wall and realized it was lunchtime. Well, he and Bonnie's lunchtime, which was after the lunch crowd was done. After he'd finish his work, they'd sit at a table in the back and share a meal, talking about whatever. He could listen to her read a phonebook with that voice of hers. And those eyes, a dark green depth that drew him in. He loved watching her blossom as she got over her shyness with him.

Pulling open the door to the Bed & Breakfast, Ray heard a cacophony of laughter flowing out of the dining room. Sandra saw him and walked over. "I'm sorry. Last minute birthday party. Bonnie said it would be at least another hour, or you can go ahead and eat without her."

He saw Bonnie moving around a hastily pulled-together long table refilling iced tea glasses. She managed to look up, see him, and smile. She gave a slight nod before turning back to what she was doing.

"Tell her I'm going for a walk. I'll be back in an hour to have a meal with her." He looked down at his light jacket. "I think I'll grab something a little heavier before I do. It's getting a bit cold out there."

"I'll tell her," Sandra said and started to the dining room. Turning back, she added, "And thanks."

He just smiled and moved down the hallway to his room. Grabbing the leather bomber jacket he's gotten from Fashion Flare, he headed to the porch. Looking down Main Street, which he'd traversed many times, he looked the other way. Now was as good a time as any to explore the other side of Ruthorford.

He bounded down the steps, waving to Miss Brenda as he headed toward the Chapel. Walking past the small Victorian-themed Chapel, he saw a cemetery next to it. Taking a slight detour from the main road, and strolled through the small cemetery, looking at a few headstones. He stopped at one. "Bill Ruthorford, Papa Ruthorford," it read. Near that one was another one that read, "Ethan Lemoyne Beauchard, beloved husband of Sandra Beauchard. Thank you for your service." He saw a few others but didn't recognize any names.

He turned and headed back to the road and away from town. He walking over a bridge that spanned a creek, figuring this had to be the creek that meandered behind the Bed & Breakfast. After about a half mile of trees and fenced pastures, he saw a small gravel road to the left. The trees grew right up next to the road, limbs arching to almost form a tunnel. He looked around. Spying no posted signs, he walked in. The trees grew bigger and older, a mix of pine and deciduous. He looked up. Bright green boughs flourished on the upper branches of a lot of the trees. So, this was where the owls got the mistletoe. A mix of mistletoe, some with red berries and some with white, decorated the trees and glistened in the filtered afternoon light.

Busy looking up, he stumbled on a root and fell forward, catching himself on the giant trunk of an ancient oak. As he looked over, he spotted the headstones, less than three feet high, small, and haphazardly placed throughout the trees. He walked through the stones, reading names, some Scottish, some Native American. He saw a relatively new one and walked over. It read Ethan Lemoyne Beauchard. That was all. He found himself looking back toward town before walking more purposefully, reading headstones. Bill Ruthorford appeared to rest under another large oak. Now, why would there be two graves? Maybe these were the fathers or grandfathers of those in the Chapel cemetery.

A sharp tingle encircled his legs, surging through his body, and he almost fell, reaching out and grabbing a headstone to steady himself. The screech of an owl came from above, and it swooped right at him, barely missing him as it dipped and flew low to the ground through the cemetery. He blinked and saw the owl chasing the outline of the creature he'd seen before. Without looking back, he blinked, turned, and ran down the gravel road until he got to the paved one. Ray didn't stop running until he was near the bridge.

Another screech sounded. He swung around and saw the owl fly from the woods straight at him. He threw out his arm in defense and, with a flutter of wings, the owl landed on his arm, its weight forcing him to struggle to hold his arm up as they stared at one another.

"Be careful what you wish for," a voice called from behind him. He turned to see Eryk and Sim running toward him.

Sim whistled, and the owl lifted its wings and flew over to Sim, landing lightly on Sim's sheathed arm. For a few seconds, Sim looked at the owl. Then, with a motion of

Sim's other hand, the owl took off and flew toward the town.

You might want to use something more than a leather jacket. Oho's talons will make short work of that jacket sleeve. Eryk translated as Sim signed.

Ray looked at his arm. Several holes pierced the leather. "I…I…I don't know what happened."

"You okay, my man?" Eryk walked over to him and looked at his eyes. They appeared dilated. "You look a little the worse for wear. Why don't we walk back with you."

"No, I'm fine. I think. I got shocked by something. Must have been a wire hanging down in that old cemetery. Then the owl." He started walking toward town.

Sim looked at Eryk as they walked behind Ray. Sim stepped forward and put his hand on Ray's shoulder, getting the images, and sending a push of energy into him. Right now, Ray needed the energy more than they needed to take any precaution. When Ray stopped and took a deep breath, Sim signed to Eryk, *Call Mike.*

Eryk took out his phone and got Mike on the first ring. "Sim and I found Ray walking just outside of the old cemetery road. He appeared confused. I think he's better now, but it might be best if you come on by. We're walking him back to the B & B." He listened for a moment. "Yep. Already done. Sim's energy push helped. We'll make sure he's hydrated."

Eryk signed to Sim. *Mike recommended the push, so we're good. Let's get him back.*

Chapter Sixteen

The walk back was slow and arduous, with the two descendants on either side of Ray helping him along. Near the Chapel, Ray's legs threatened to give out, and the two each grabbed an arm, holding him up. Ray refused to be carried, though Sim had Eryk reassure him he could do it with ease.

Bonnie had just finished and was stepping out of the dining room when they walked in, barely keeping Ray on his feet.

"What happened?" She rushed over, laying her hand on his arm. His pulse was thready and his blood pressure was high. They started to move and she held up her hand, stopping them. She closed her eyes—she didn't want him seeing her eyes—concentrated, and set his rhythm to hers. Satisfied he would make it down the hall without collapsing, she stepped back and looked at him.

"Thank you," he said, his voice low and hoarse, as he looked deep into her eyes before letting Sim and Eryk guide him down the hall.

They'd just gotten him on the bed when Mike walked in behind Bonnie.

"I steadied him," Bonnie said. "Pulse's a bit thready. Blood pressure's high. Eyes dilated."

Mike stepped around her to the bed and placed his hand against Ray's neck. Clammy. He took his blood pressure. It was stable. Pulse normal. He looked into his eyes.

"Can you tell me what happened?"

"Not sure," he said, trying to concentrate. "I went for a walk. Found this old cemetery. I think I tripped over a root. There must have been a downed wire because I felt this strong shock, like it wrapped around my legs. I ran. I wanted to make sure I got to the road before I collapsed. Then, Sim and Eryk found me."

"What were you doing that far away?" Mike asked.

"I decided to take a walk while I waited for Bonnie." He sat up. "Wait. The owl. He landed on me…I think."

Bonnie broke open a bottle of water and handed it to Mike.

"Here. Drink this." He put the bottle in Ray's hand, watching him try to grip the bottle. "Maybe we should take you to the clinic and run some tests."

"No!" It came out more forcefully than he'd have liked. "Sorry. I feel a lot better. I'm so tired of being a pin cushion."

"Do you think you could eat something light?"

"Funny, right now I feel like I could eat a horse. But I'll settle for something lighter." He offered a smile.

Sim smiled at Eryk, both aware that hunger was a typical side effect of a strong push.

"How about I make us some plates and bring them back? We can have an early dinner here," Bonnie suggested.

"I'd like that. Mike, seriously, I feel fine. I admit it knocked me on my ass. Probably ought to have someone check that out. But I'll be fine."

"I'm sure Eryk can get someone to take care of it," Mike reassured Ray, glancing at Eryk. He knew damned well there was no downed power line in the cemetery. "Bonnie, I think you should keep him company for a little while. I've got to get back." He put his instruments back in his bag. "I'll check on you later tonight."

"I'll go get us a tray and tell Sandra." She looked at Eryk.

"I think I'll just keep him company until you get back, Bonnie," Eryk answered her silent question and sat down at the table. "May I," he asked Ray, nodding at the sketchbook.

"Sure. Mostly therapy exercises."

Sim signed, *You take care. I'm here if you need me,* having Eryk interpret for him.

"Thanks for everything, Sim. I do envy your friendship with that gorgeous owl."

Get better and I'll introduce you properly, he signed while Eryk spoke.

"I'd like that...I think."

Sim smiled and nodded, following Mike out.

Mike stopped in the lobby. "Want to tell me what really happened. Or, is this descendant business?"

Sim nodded.

Resigned, Mike sighed. "Okay, call a meeting and text me when. I'll be there. I'll tell Teresa."

"Teresa's upstairs with Aby," Bonnie said. "I'll go get him something to eat." She saw Mike's expression. "I know, nothing too heavy. I've got some roasted chicken in the kitchen, parsley potatoes, and green beans. On the light side."

"That's my girl. Thanks, Bonnie."

Mike watched Bonnie head toward the dining room and Sim out the front doors. Descendants. The most gifted people he'd ever met and the nicest. Even Ethan, who'd definitely had issues, had turned out doing the right thing. Too bad they had to keep such a low profile. He knew only too well how the rest of the world dealt with people who were different. Sadly, history hadn't changed that much in millennia. He had no idea what the future held, but he knew whatever it was, they would face it together.

Mike hit the button to the fourth floor and found himself smiling, thinking about his wife and daughter up there waiting for him. Ruthorford had been his whole life for most of his life since he'd become a doctor. He didn't regret any of it, even that time when Teresa had been lured away from him. He had her back now and an amazing and beautiful daughter to boot. The elevator opened to the peals of laughter coming from the library, and he saw Teresa lying on the floor with Aby on top of her, giggling for all she was worth.

"There are my girls," he called out.

Aby wiggled her way off her mom and ran toward him as fast as her little legs would carry her. "Dad-dy!"

Yes, his life was about as complete as it could be.

***

"I hope there's something good to eat at the B & B. I'm starving, and this is definitely cutting into my dinner prep time," Jasmine complained as she looked around the table at Teresa, Mike, John, Eryk, Sim, Dorian, and Morgan."

"You weren't planning to cook, anyway," Eyrk laughed.

"I could have," Jasmine defended.

"Meatloaf," Teresa stated. "Mashed potatoes and peas."

"Good," Jasmine said, sending Eryk a look.

"My favorite," Eryk said.

"Food is your favorite," Jasmine said.

Morgan put an antipasto platter on the table and smiled at Jasmine. "Wouldn't want you starving to death."

"You put in those large black olives. I love you," Jasmine said, popping one in her mouth.

Jenn's voice rose over the speaker of the phone on the table. "Hey, guys, can we stop talking about food. Martha is visiting her sister, and I'm stuck with leftovers."

"I'll bring home some goodies," John said. "I promise."

"Thank you," Jenn said. "Okay, I've been doing some research. I know we've been worried a bit about Ray's mother being in Cultural Anthropology. Her specialty is Anthropological Linguistics. Her emphasis is the study of Ocracoke's Brogue. Kinda fascinating," she said, catching herself before she got carried away. "Anyway, I don't think it would be too much of an issue if it slipped. Can't say she wouldn't be intrigued, but we aren't primarily her interest."

"What about the NDA?" John asked.

"I've got the non-disclosure written up in case you decide to go that route."

"Given what Sim's been telling us, I don't see what choice we have," Dorian said. "That creature seems to have an interest in Ray. Three times are too many times to be a coincidence. And Oho has taken to protecting him. Also, either because of the size of the creature or some unique attributes, Ray is being affected. We have to find a way to get rid of it," Dorian stated. "It's not coming back here. It was at the old cemetery."

"I know I'm a little behind," Jenn interjected, "but just what have you been planning?"

"I think they realized I was right," Jasmine said. "That thing may actually be trying to go back through that opening but can't."

"So," she added, "if we are going to tell Ray, for his own safety and sanity, I might add, we might as well see if he's willing to be the bait."

"Could you be any colder?" Teresa said, admonishing her cousin.

Jasmine looked at Teresa. "I'm not being cold. I deal with intakes all the time at Safe Harbor, women struggling to just survive and be safe from the monsters they unknowingly took into their lives. I understand that, if that thing stays around him, it can be dangerous, not only to him but to other non-descendants, like Mike," she added for emphasis. "But we aren't going to let that happen. And the easiest way to not let that happen is for Ray to help attract it to the site where it can go through. In order to do that, we must tell Ray that what we've let him believe are hallucinations are very real. Consequently, we have to tell him about Ruthorford and the descendants and hope he won't tell anyone." Jasmine stopped and took a breath. "Do I have that about right?" Her voice came out sharp and her eyes flashed.

She was met with silence. "At least I didn't sugarcoat it," she said. "We go through so much every day to keep our secrets safe. And we do a damned good job. Eryk and I live among his magician's troupe and, so far," she knocked on the table, "no one knows. Or, if they do, they aren't letting us know they know."

Teresa reached out and covered Jasmine's hand with her own, trying to send a push and felt resistance, Jasmine holding back. Teresa looked at her, gave her a simple nod. Jasmine looked down and turned her hand over, joining their hands. Images filled Teresa's mind, making her heart ache. She squeezed Jasmine's hand.

"I'm sorry," Jasmine said. "I just wanted this holiday to be different. It seems like every time I turn around, we're dealing with the outside. So far, in just a few years, we've had some weird government pocket agency coming after Di, militia extremists trying to take us out, and drones snooping—I don't think that's completely over, by the way. It's always something." What she'd failed to mention was her own kidnapping and assault. She didn't have to. It was in everyone's mind.

Eryk put his arm around Jasmine. "Why don't you sit this one out?" He asked gently.

"No." She straightened. "I don't want Morgan and Dorian in danger, not with the twins."

Sim signed, *They don't have to be. In fact, I think the perfect setup would be Eryk matched with me. We both have combined abilities, which gives us the advantage of shifting our energy if we need to.*

Jasmine looked at Eryk. He nodded, squeezing her shoulder. Tears overflowed from her dark eyes. She sniffled and swiped at them. Eryk took her hand and softly kissed her palm. "Let us take care of it. Besides, you need to get back to Virginia and finish that case."

"I don't know."

Eryk's voice was firm. "Jenn?"

"Plane is sitting at Coweta airport and can fly her back tonight. I just heard from Kayla. They were able to get the children away from him, and they are at Safe Harbor with their mom. He's in jail. Bail was denied."

That made up Jasmine's mind; she'd been on the phone off and on all day, navigating the bureaucracy from a distance. "Oh, thank God. Please tell the pilot I'll be there in a couple of hours."

Eryk stood. "You all figure things out. I'm going to take Jasmine home and then take her to the airport. I'll check in later." He looked at Sim, "We've got this, my friend."

Teresa hugged Jasmine and gave her more energy. "You get some rest, too. We love you."

Jasmine nodded and started toward the door when she turned back. "Look, guys, I'm sorry I've been a bitch. You know that's how I handle stress. You really are the best."

"We love you, Jasmine. Go, take care of that family," Morgan said.

She nodded, turned, and put her hand in Eryk's, letting him lead her out.

"With all she's been through, do you really think doing what she does is good for her?" Dorian asked.

Jenn spoke up. "No one could do it better. She knows firsthand what can happen and how to survive."

"Well, even though we didn't like the way she put it, she was right," John said. "I don't know if it will go as smoothly as it did with someone like Ozzy. I mean, after all, it turned out he was a descendant."

Mike spoke up. "Ray's analysis shows possible Scottish ancestry, but not strong, not like a descendant's. I want to examine him again first. Then, if I agree, you can set up a meeting. He seemed a bit confused earlier. He needs to fully understand what we are telling him, especially if we're asking him to sign an NDA. I don't know how he'll feel about leaving out his family. I think Teresa and I should talk to him first. He might feel more comfortable knowing I'm a non-descendant. Then, and only then, we can bring him here for more discussion. One step at a time."

Everyone at the table nodded. They never took it lightly when another person had to be brought into their secret. So far, like with the militia extremists, no one believed the stories because Ethan disavowed everything, and they had been the epitome of "normal," boringly so, since that occurred.

***

"Did you have enough to eat?" Bonnie asked, eyeing that half-eaten plate in front of Ray.

"I'm sorry, Bonnie. I know it's amazing. I just don't feel much like eating. One minute I'm starving and the next not so much."

She started to reach out to lay her hand on his arm, and he pulled it back, putting his hands in his lap. "I'm sorry. I know you are trying to help me, but I want to do it myself."

She nodded, put her hands in her lap, and looked down at her plate.

"Don't do that. Please. Just because I question something, I'm not criticizing you. I really do appreciate all you have done for me. I'm just trying to think some things out. For some reason, my mind is a little fuzzy about what happened at that cemetery."

Bonnie didn't say anything, just watched him.

"There's a cemetery by that little church. Then, there's that one in the woods."

"That's the original cemetery. When they built the Chapel, they wanted a cemetery near it." That wasn't exactly a lie.

He frowned. "I walked through there. That's where Teresa's first husband is buried and, I think I saw a marker for Sandra's husband."

Bonnie nodded.

"Well, that one sure is a lot prettier than the one in the woods. Looks like that one hasn't been cared for in a while." He stopped, scrunching up his eyes, thinking.

"I've got it. I remember."

Bonnie's heart skipped a beat.

"I saw it when I went in."

Bonnie held her breath.

He leaned forward, excited. "All the mistletoe in the trees. It's beautiful. That must be where Oho got the mistletoe he brought the other day." As if realization suddenly struck him, he grinned. "That has to be what he was doing in there. Getting mistletoe. I must have startled him when I tripped over the wire. And he certainly startled me. I ran. He came after me." He sat back, smiling.

Bonnie smiled back at him and hoped Mike would come back soon.

Chapter Seventeen

As a surprise, Sandra brought two cups of custard pudding to Bonnie and Ray, along with some spiced tea, declaring this would set everything back to perfect.

She hadn't been far wrong. The banter became lighter as they turned on the television, watching reruns of the original Star Trek, realizing they were both secret Trekkies.

Mike walked in to find them on the bed, laughing and watching TV. Truth was, the only way Bonnie could get Ray to lie down was if she piled up on the bed with him. She'd grabbed all the extra pillows out of the closet, so they were sitting against clouds of comfort, telling him how she and her sister still did it to this day. Their favorite was watching black and white scary movies, like Frankenstein or Dracula.

"Well, I can see you are doing much better," Mike said with a chuckle.

Bonnie started to hop off the bed, and Mike held up his hand, glancing over his shoulder at the TV screen. "Stay. I just want to take a peek at Ray. If Teresa wasn't waiting for me, I swear I'd cozy right up there with you. I loved Star Trek."

Bonnie scooted back against the pillows and watched Mike make fast work of the exam. "Any headache?"

Ray shook his head.

"Nausea?"

"Nope. I tell you, I'm fine."

Bonnie glanced at her watch. "In that case, if Mike says it's okay, I'd better skedaddle. I need to help Sandra close up, at least."

"But I don't want you to go," Ray said, exaggerating a pout.

"Hey, you get some sleep and we'll have breakfast together. Cartoons included," Bonnie said and gathered the dishes, put them on the tray, and headed to the door.

Mike stepped over and opened it. "If you run into Teresa, tell her I'll be upstairs, waiting on that pie."

"Will do. Nite nite, y'all," Bonnie said as she left.

Mike turned and saw the grin on Ray's face. "I recognize that look," he teased. "Ruthorford women can get under your skin fast. They are pretty special."

"I get your message. Handle with care."

"I've known her damned near all of her life. She's like a daughter, if you get my drift."

"Message received. Wouldn't matter. I care too much about her to risk doing anything that might hurt her. And, trust me, that's a difficult promise to keep. She's so…so…delectable."

"I'll be honest, you've been good for her. She became more introverted as she got older. You've brought her out. I haven't seen her that carefree," he nodded to the bed, "since she was a little girl."

"Thanks for telling me that. Her friendship means a lot to me."

"Good. You might also remember Sim, Eryk, and Dorian are like brothers. Very big, very tough brothers."

Ray laughed. "Yes, sir."

"Good, then I'm going to head on upstairs to my own daughter, who I will promptly lock away when she hits puberty. You get some sleep. I'll talk with you tomorrow."

***

The early morning light filtered over the back lawn, sending long shadows across frost-edged leaves. Ray wasn't sure which was more beautiful, the scene outside or the gorgeous green-eyed woman sitting across from him in the dining room.

"Cheese blintzes for breakfast. I feel like a king." He cut into the tender wrap and lifted it to his mouth, apple and cinnamon flavoring the light whipped cheese.

"My favorite, too. I'm glad Teresa let me loose in the kitchen."

"Well, you did make enough for them, as well," he whispered and nodded toward the couple sitting a few tables away.

Bonnie chuckled. "Yeah, I didn't see either one of them complaining."

"Do you ever get a day off?" he asked as he drank some of the coffee he was fast becoming addicted to.

"Not often. Between here and the boutique, I stay pretty busy." She looked up at Ray, his golden eyes still as mesmerizing as they'd been the first time she'd seen them. "To be honest, I never had much desire to take time off."

"I'm flattered, I think."

"You should be. Ray, you've been good for me. Thank you."

"Thank you. I've never known a woman like you. So genuine."

The fork stopped midway to Bonnie's mouth, and she put it down, slowly pushing back her chair, the smile gone. "I better get back to work," she said, not looking up. "Thanks for breakfast."

Ray pushed back his chair, a frown forming.

"Don't get up. You take your time. I'll bring you more coffee."

"Bonnie, what...?" But his words fell on her retreating back.

Ray sat there, going over their conversation, not knowing what he'd said but knowing that something had caused her to withdraw.

His mind kept going back to the cemetery. Something was nagging at his memory, but it just wouldn't come forward. Must be that damned Covid. He'd read about long Covid and brain fog. Some days his mind was clear as glass, and on others, things just didn't make sense.

Mike stood up from his table. When Teresa nodded, he walked over to Ray. "Would you do me a favor and come up to the fourth floor when you get done? Teresa and I would like to talk with you."

Ray pushed away his plate. "How about now? I seemed to have lost my appetite." His eyes went to the kitchen door.

Bonnie stepped through the kitchen door to see Ray following Mike to the elevator. She couldn't help it, tears formed in her eyes. She turned and went back into the kitchen, Teresa on her heels.

"I need you and Sandra to watch the lobby and the dining room for a while." She put her hand on Bonnie's arm and, after receiving her feelings, pushed warm energy to her. "It's got to be done. You know that."

Bonnie nodded and swallowed down her sadness, knowing inside that, after they talked to Ray, everything would change. At least she'd had the last few weeks, a time she would remember forever.

After Teresa left, Sandra walked over and took Bonnie in her arms. "I wish I could tell you it would be okay. I can't. But I can tell you that, no matter what, we'll get you through it."

Bonnie's voice came out barely above a whisper as she tried to smile, "I know. Thank you." She pulled away and started prepping more blintz batter.

Ray followed Mike down the hallway and stepped into the massive library, sunlight falling on mahogany shelves filled with books.

"Coffee?" Jenn asked as he walked in.

"No thanks. I'm good."

"Uncle Mike?"

"None for me, thanks."

She fixed a mug, handed it to John, and made one for herself.

"Have a seat," Mike indicated a large round library table to the side of the fireplace.

By the time they were seated, Teresa walked in and joined them.

Jenn pulled some papers out of a manila envelope. "Ray, before we can tell you anything, we have to have you sign an NDA, non—"

"Non-disclosure agreement," he finished for her. "I'm familiar with them." Then he thought for a few seconds. "Can't tell you why, but I am."

"Okay. Would you have any opposition to signing one with the Abbott House Foundation?"

"As long as it doesn't involve anything illegal," he said, trying to keep it light, even though his nerves had jacked up. For a second, he wished Bonnie was with him.

John chuckled. "Jenn is our Legal Counsel, and I am the Chief of Police and our tribal representative. I can assure you, there's nothing illegal. We are asking you to keep our secrets to yourself. Only yourself."

"I'm intrigued." Then, he laughed. "So, in order to satisfy my curiosity, I need to sign."

"Pretty much."

"Got a pen?"

Jenn held onto the pen as she spoke, "I need to let you know that you have been thoroughly vetted, as has your family. Yet, we are still asking that you not divulge what we tell you, even with them."

He only hesitated a moment before taking the pen. With a flourish, he signed Lucas Raymond Grissom and pushed the document back to her.

She had John and Teresa witness it, then slipped it into her valise before nodding to Mike.

"It's hard to know where to start. However, I think it's more important to start with what affects you personally." Mike took a deep breath and let it out. "First of all, those creatures you've seen are real."

It took a moment for Ray to put his mind around what he'd heard. "You mean I'm not hallucinating?"

"No. We're not sure why you can see them. Up to this point, only certain descendants can see them."

"Descendants?"

Mike shook his head. "This gets more convoluted by the moment. "I know you got a short history lesson about the Scots and the Native Americans. Their progeny, at least as pertains to here, are called descendants. They are born with enhanced abilities."

"What kind of abilities?"

"Let's just say many use a bit more than 10% of their brains. And some have the ability to see the Gulatega, creatures that come through a dimensional portal."

Ray listened, then let out a nervous laugh. "Wait. Dimensional portals?" When Mike started to speak, Ray held up his hand. "Suddenly, I have about a thousand things going through my head, so let's keep it simple. This creature. Why can I see it? I don't think I'm either Scot or Native American."

"You do have some Scot but not the combination the descendants have. Sim thinks it's the tetrachromacy. He can see them, and he has it." Mike left out that Sim had more abilities than anyone in Ruthorford.

Jenn reached down in her case and pulled out some pages. "These are drawings of what the Gulatega, as we've known it, looks like. This is the drawing you made. It appears somewhat different and much bigger."

"Long ago, Native Americans discovered them on this mountain," John said. "The snowy owls would come and warn them when the creatures roamed. Those creatures have a neurological effect on humans—like dementia. When the Native Americans and Scots got together, their progeny's combined abilities enabled them to open a portal, sending the creatures through. Those gifted with this ability are called GateKeepers. As long as there are GateKeepers in Ruthorford, the creatures stay away."

"We haven't seen one in quite a while. The one you saw is much larger and can't get through the normal portal. It seems attracted to you. But, luckily, so is Oho, who keeps protecting you from it."

At that moment, Dorian and Morgan stepped into the library. "Our Gatekeepers," Teresa said, nodding to the two.

Ray smiled at them. "Oho's protecting me? You mean this brain fog I seem to be having could be because of the creature?"

Mike nodded. "Possibly. We're not sure."

"The old cemetery," Ray started and ran his fingers through his hair, "it wasn't a downed line. It was that creature, wasn't it?"

"Yes. There is a large portal in that cemetery," Dorian said. "But we haven't been able to open it. It has different harmonics or something. We think that may be where it came from or is trying to get through."

"I think I'd like that coffee now," Ray said.

Morgan walked over to the buffet, fixed a mug, walked back, and held it out. When he reached for it, she held on, and as his fingers covered hers, she blinked and looked at him, then blinked and stepped back. "He's fine."

Ray studied her face. "Your eyes."

She offered him a sweet smile.

"I've seen them before. Hell, I've seen them on myself."

"What?" Mike said.

"I don't know if it happens all the time anymore, but it has been when I've blinked and my color vision shifts, my eyes appear to take on that swirling thing. That's when I can see the creature."

"I want you to do that now," Morgan said. "Take my hand." She held out her hand as she stood from sitting on the arm of the couch.

Ray stood and walked around the table, taking Morgan's hand. He closed his eyes and concentrated. When he opened them, he saw her in colors radiating outward. She pulled her hand away and the colors diminished, his color vision becoming tetrachromatic only.

He closed his eyes and opened them again. Everyone was normal. He dropped down on the edge of the couch, a bit woozy. Teresa stepped over and put her hand on his arm, giving him a push. He instantly felt better.

"Thanks," he said, coming to grips with the energy pushes she'd been giving. "This vision thing is different and I'm not used to it. This time it was different still." He looked at Morgan. "You are even more beautiful than…." His eyes went to Dorian. "Sorry. I've never seen anything like it. It does feel a bit intimate, now that I think about it."

"I can't do that," Dorian said. "And I'd prefer you not do it again on my wife without invitation."

"Absolutely." He felt color infuse his neck.

"I do it to read health auras," Morgan explained. "What I see may be different from what you are seeing."

"Do all descendants take on that swirling effect?" he asked, thinking of Bonnie.

"No," John said. "We are all different. I am pure Native American—that I know of, but I have the ability to calm…all species."

Teresa handed Ray his coffee and he took a big swallow. "Mike and Jenn are non-descendants. By our bylaws, the head of the Abbott House in Atlanta has to be." Teresa reached out and took Mike's hand. "Mike accepted an offer to become a small-town doctor—not knowing what he was getting into—and, fortunately for us, stayed."

"Best decision I ever made," Mike said, giving Teresa's hand a gentle squeeze.

The look between them said it all.

Looking around the room, Ray smiled a somewhat crooked smile. "I'm going to extrapolate from what you've told me. Since that creature appears to be drawn to me, you want me to lead it to the old cemetery so you can get it to go through that portal, right?"

"Yes," Dorian said, his look very serious. "However, Morgan and I won't be opening the portal. We've already found we can't. Even Eryk and Jasmine can't. Eryk and Sim are going to try since they are stronger and have the most variations in their abilities. We are hoping they can do it. I have to be honest. We don't know if they can, and we don't know what effect that creature can have on you that close."

Mike watched Ray take it all in and give a slow nod as he thought it out. "You are taking this awfully well," Mike said, a hint of cynicism in his tone.

Ray looked up at him, a big smile forming. "Hey, I'm not hallucinating!"

That brought laughter across the room.

"Seriously. It was happening over and over, and then I saw my eyes swirl like I'd thought I'd seen Sim's and Bonnie's and felt these tingles when people touched me—more than static. I've got static. What you all and that creature have is not static. Then Mike tells me about that syndrome—"

"Charles Bonnet," Mike interjected.

"…and I thought I was losing my mind. Or I'd have to live with it." He looked around the room. "Trust me, this I can live with."

He turned and looked at Mike. "Plus, I will never be able to thank you enough for what you've given back to me. I came here to heal and come to terms with what doctors told me would be my altered life. It's not. The tinnitus and the headaches are gone, and I can use my hand. You've given me back my life, albeit a bit enhanced," he added and laughed. "But, most of all, you have given me back my art, which was my life, until Covid. Coming to Ruthorford was the best thing that ever happened to me. So, helping you get rid of this creature is a small payment for what I've received. Tell me what I can do to help you remove this creature."

Dorian had moved over to the table and was leafing through the pictures. "First, you could use your art to give us the best picture you can of this thing, if you remember."

"Not a probably. Oh, I remember. Especially now that I don't think I should be forgetting."

Jenn spoke up. "I need to remind you about confidentiality, Ray. I'm sorry. But we need our privacy protected."

"I understand. I'm assuming Gillian doesn't know."

Teresa shook her head. "No. We host writers' groups all the time. We have fairs. We do a lot with the outside. And, when we do, we are very careful. That is why that creature has to be gotten rid of. It has a horrible effect on non-descendants."

"Even my people," John added.

"Then, we will. One way or the other." Ray said, confident. "And I will honor your trust."

He stood. "I have a favor to ask. I would like some time to talk to Bonnie. Please."

Teresa stood. "That we can give you." She looked around the room. "There are enough here to cover her for a few hours. I'll go down with you, so she'll go. And, thank you."

"No. Thank all of you," he said and headed toward the hall.

Chapter Eighteen

Teresa hustled into the kitchen, where Bonnie, once again, was scrubbing down the counters, nerves showing. "Go. Take off that apron, fluff your hair, and get out of here. Ray's waiting," she said and pulled the scrunchie from Bonnie's mass of sable hair. "Shake your head."

Bonnie did as directed and Teresa smiled. "Don't know a man yet that can resist a woman with slightly mussed hair." She pulled her in for a tight hug and turned her toward the door. "Don't worry. Everything's fine," she said, giving her a slight shove out the door. She stepped into the dining room as Morgan, Dorian, Jenn, and John walked in. She almost turned back when Morgan called out. "We're taking over for a while. Go."

At that moment, Ray stepped into the dining room doorway with a smile that stopped her in her tracks, and she couldn't do anything but smile back and walk toward him.

He took her hand. "Your place or mine? I want to talk."

"Mine. More privacy and more food options without having everyone and their brother descending upon us."

Mike stepped off the elevator as Teresa walked to the counter in the lobby. Both of them watched Bonnie and Ray head across the street to her apartment. He walked over, picked up his bag from behind the counter, and turned to his wife. "As much as I don't want to, I need to go to the clinic."

"Ever thought about retiring?" She said as her lips played across his.

"And be under your feet all day. Not a chance." He laughed, kissed her once more, and headed out the door.

Bonnie led Ray inside the apartment over the boutique and closed the door. "Coffee?" She asked, turning on the pod coffee maker.

"I think I'm about coffee'd out," he said, turning her to face him in the small kitchen. "First, I want to do this." His eyes caught hers and held, then moved to her lips before his head lowered to hers, capturing the warm softness he craved.

She felt her heart swell and eased her arms around his neck, settling against his hard body. As his arms tightened, the kiss deepened, and his tongue stroked hers, his breath joining with hers, pulling them into desire that weaved through and around them.

He finally pulled back, resting his head against hers, breathing hard. "Now might be a good time to adjust my pulse," he whispered, joking.

"Can't," she said, breathy. "Mine's going faster than yours."

"We're doomed," he choked and took her mouth again, letting the desire consume them.

When he pulled back, he looked at her swollen lips and felt his knees weaken. "It's a good thing I don't really know where the bedroom is."

"It's—"

"Please, God, don't tell me. I'm hanging on by a thread here."

Bonnie laughed, slipped her arms around his waist, and hugged him tight before letting go. She turned, opened the fridge, and pulled out two cans of Coke. "Here. You wanted to talk, remember?"

He took the can and rested it against his forehead. "Yeah. That." He pulled the tab and let the liquid run down his throat, the cold burning through his hot body. "Woman, you have no idea what you are doing to me."

"It's a descendant thing," she laughed and stopped. "You did have the descendant discussion, didn't you?" She turned and looked at him, worry showing on her face.

"Yes. But not that particular topic. What? Are you telling me descendants have some sort of animal magnetism us mere mortals can't resist?"

She laughed and plopped down on the sofa. "Only with other descendants," she said.

"But, I'm not a descendant," he said and sat next to her.

She just shrugged and took a drink of her Coke. "Let's table that discussion until another time."

He looked toward the hallway that most likely led to the bedroom. "Let's not wait too long, okay?"

She shoved him with her shoulder. "Okay. Tell me what happened at the meeting."

Ray gave her a rundown of the meeting, starting with him signing the NDA and finishing with a discussion of the creature and Morgan scanning him.

"When I saw her—I guess it was kind of her aura, I was amazed. It's so beautiful. I said so. Dorian didn't really appreciate it." He laughed, turning to her. "I saw your eyes swirl. Are you like Morgan?"

Bonnie looked down. This was harder than she realized. She'd always hated being a descendant, and this made her extremely nervous, almost panicky.

He watched her, then turned and raised her chin with his fingers until she looked into his eyes. "What's wrong?"

"I just…I don't get all excited about being different, is all." He wouldn't let her look down, though she wanted to.

"Me, either," he said.

When her eyes latched onto his, he spoke, "Can you imagine a kid trying to explain what he sees, the colors he sees, that are so different from everyone else's? It's frustrating and sets one up for bullying. At least you grew up being accepted, no matter what difference there was."

She automatically reached out, putting her hand on his arm, steadying his pulse. She pulled back. "Sorry. It's automatic."

"See. You can't help it any more than I could. When Covid took it, I was almost glad. Then my art was gone, and the headaches and tinnitus were debilitating. You all have given all that back to me, plus. It's different now, but it may be better. I can see what others see now, not just what I see."

"I'm glad, then."

"I know you saw the creature that day in the alley."

"I only saw it because you were holding me. Before, I could see what Sim saw in your body because he was touching me. I can't do it on my own."

Ray thought back. "That's when I first saw your and Sim's eyes swirling."

She nodded. "The only thing I seem to be able to do is to adjust body rhythms."

"Would you be willing to try an experiment?"

"What?"

He stood and held out his hand. She took it and stood in front of him. He took her other hand and closed his eyes. "Try not to adjust our rhythms," he chuckled. "I want to try something."

"Okay." She watched as he frowned, concentrating before he opened his eyes. The gold color took on a swirling effect. Her sharp intake told him what she'd seen.

He looked into her eyes. They, too, seemed to have the effect. He let his gaze move down her body, and she did the same. "Oh, my God, you are gorgeous," he said.

"So are you," she breathed. "I've never seen anything like it. Not even with Sim."

He released one of her hands and walked toward the mirror over the small buffet, almost falling over an ottoman. "Kind of hard to maneuver this way," he chuckled.

They stood side by side in front of the mirror. Their eyes had a similar appearance and their colors were heightened, but they didn't see the auras. "Interesting," he said. "That's what I normally would see before Covid."

They turned and looked at one another, seeing the auras.

"I wonder why it doesn't translate in a reflection?"

"I have no idea, but I have to stop. I'm a little woozy," Bonnie said and sat in the chair next to the buffet.

He kneeled down in front of her. "I'm sorry. I guess I'm getting better at it. I felt that way at Teresa's. Here, take my hand and match your rhythm to mine."

She did and he closed his eyes, returning the vision to normal. He leaned over and pulled one of the Cokes from the table. "Sip this."

"Thanks. I'm better," she said, taking a deep breath.

"What about your sister? She seems so different from you."

"She is. She is extraverted and afraid of nothing. Her talent, as we call it, is her ability to soothe, which is weird because she has so much energy. That's why she takes care of our mother. She also has this incredible sense of order, hence her love of the Fashion Flare. I just seem to adjust rhythms." She shrugged.

"And have a siren's voice," he added.

"I never thought of that as a talent," she grinned.

"You should. I have my art. I discovered it as an escape and a way to show others about my vision without saying anything."

"I love your art."

He stood. "Speaking of art. I'm going to run down to the gallery and get some supplies. I want you to help me create a really good picture of that creature for them. I think, between what we both saw and our combined talent, we can help them."

"I probably should head back," she stood, not sure how she could help. Her ability was based on his.

"Nope. Teresa already told me you were free. I need your help, Bonnie. Please."

"Okay. I brought some BBQ home yesterday. Want a BBQ sandwich?"

"Oh, yeah. That stuff's amazing. Which reminds me, another of your talents, as you call them, is your amazing ability with food. Just saying." With that, he turned and went out the door.

She heard his footfalls on the steps and went into the kitchen to fix them something to eat, hoping to get her mind off of his lips, his eyes—when they weren't swirling, his wavy dark blonde hair, and that body. Oh, that body. Those jeans, low on his hips and the way they hugged his ass. She shook her head. They definitely needed to have a discussion before they made it to that bedroom. Bonnie opened the fridge and grabbed the BBQ, potato salad, and coleslaw, determined to refocus her mind.

Ray wasn't doing much better, trying to concentrate on the tools he needed to create the picture of a monster instead of focusing on the soft curves that lay beneath those tight jeans and angora sweater.

"Here to work?"

KC's voice startled him and he jumped. "Sorry, I didn't know anyone was here. "No, I'm getting some things I need to do a drawing of…." Suddenly, his words trailed off before he said 'the creature,' not knowing where she stood, if she was a descendant or an outsider, like himself.

She walked over and leaned against the wall. "I'm married to John's brother, Rowe. Remember? I know about Ruthorford and the Gulatega."

He stacked pencils and the watercolor pens on a large sketchbook. "Not trusted a couple of hours and I almost blew it."

"You won't. It gets easier with time."

"Are you—"

"Sort of," she interrupted. Miss Brenda is my aunt. My talent seems to be in my art. Long story. I was here when I was young, left for a long time, and returned. Found my home and my love."

"These people. This place. It's amazing."

"Trust me when I tell you they've got your back."

"I think I know that."

"Good. Let me know if there's anything I can do to help," she called out as he made his way to the back door.

"Hey. Just the fact that KC offered to help me—just did. Thanks. You made my day."

"Well, that was easy," she said, laughing. "Take care."

By the time Ray got back inside Bonnie's apartment, he could smell the BBQ. She'd set up places at the small table by the front windows. He set his stuff down on a chair and walked over. "This smells so good. Thank you."

"We'll eat, then clear the table, and you can work there."

"Sounds like a plan," he said, taking a bite of the sandwich. "Best BBQ I've ever had."

Bonnie finished chewing and wiped her mouth. "It's a take on Carolina BBQ. I tweaked Bill's recipe a little. Everyone seems to enjoy it. That's all that matters."

"This is smoked. I didn't see a smoker behind the B & B."

"Bill actually built a stone room off of the back of the kitchen. A mini smokehouse. The smokers are on the back wall. It keeps the smells from fouling other things in the kitchen, and we can keep it going for large gatherings. You ought to try the brisket."

They finished eating and Bonnie cleared away the dishes as Ray started sketching out what he remembered about the creature. It took a moment of looking back. He'd been so determined to make it a hallucination, he wanted to make sure he wasn't embellishing what he'd actually seen.

"Elongate the eyes a little," Bonnie said, watching him do his magic. "I couldn't tell if those were ears or horns," she said. Try ears." He made the changes.

"Weird, I didn't notice a tail on the one by the creek."

"There was definitely one on the creature in the cemetery. Damn, I hope there isn't more than one." Their eyes met and they both shook their heads.

"Oho seemed to be after one. The other owls aren't joining, so I'm guessing there aren't more," Bonnie said, pulling the chair around and sitting closer to him. "That's great. You know, I felt like there was more substance to it, that we couldn't see. And, that thing on its side," she said, pointing to the sketch, "it was folded more."

"Like a wing?"

"Um-hmmm." She watched him make changes. "Too much. Up more toward the shoulder."

"You really got a good look."

"From when it moved away from you and looked back. Then, Oho started chasing it down toward the creek. I guess its tail could have been wrapped to the side. Can you add something to give it a sense of size?" she asked.

He sketched a bit. "How about this?" It was a cemetery stone beside it and Oho near.

"That's it!" Bonnie said. "No wonder it won't go through the portal. From what I've heard, that portal in the cottage is really small."

"What cottage?"

"The one behind The Shoppe of Spells. I've never seen the portal, but I've heard about it. There was an incident right after Morgan got here. Her real parents had been killed, and the attorneys thought she knew she'd been adopted. That in itself was a fiasco. Anyway, talk about a trial by fire. Poor thing had no idea about any of this, and suddenly she's a GateKeeper. With Dorian's love and help, she stepped up. Also saved Meadow, John's cousin, using her aura vision, got her help in time."

Ray started to ask questions, and Bonnie held up her hand. We have a lot of history here. Take it slow. Let's deal with what we're dealing with here and now. How are they going to get it through?"

"They're going to try to open the portal in the old cemetery."

Bonnie blanched. "But that's the Ghost Walker portal."

Ray had been working on the sketch and stopped, turning to her. "And just what is the Ghost Walker portal?"

"Well, it's just a story and folklore, but that old cemetery is where they actually bury the descendants. There was a story about a couple of kids seeing a "ghost," she made air quotes, "going into the portal from the cemetery. Kinda like the essence of the descendants or something."

From the look on his face, she stopped. "Ray, just how *are* they planning on getting that thing to go through the portal?" She put her hand on his arm and felt his pulse racing. This time she didn't calm him.

"Me," he said slowly and quietly.

Bonnie jumped up. "Oh, no. No way in hell!"

At that moment, Ray's phone beeped. He pulled it out of his pocket and read the text.

<Meeting on for tonight. 7. At the Shoppe. Tell Bonnie she's covered if she wants to come with you.> It was from Dorian.

He read her the text.

"Damn straight, I'm coming with you. You are *not* going to be their guinea pig! I don't give a shit how beholden you feel toward them." She paced across the room.

Ray got up and reached out to stop her. Damn, what fire she had. Her eyes nearly flashed. He smiled at her, and she started on again. "They don't have any right to ask—"

He shut her up the only way he knew how, capturing her mouth with his. By the time he finished, her eyes had gone from flashing to dreamy, and her heartbeat, although fast, matched his, strong and steady.

Chapter Nineteen

They took their time walking to The Shoppe of Spells, walking down Main Street, crossing over in front of Sandra and Ozzy's place, then coming back up by way of Elements. All the windows were outlined in lights, and wreaths hung on doors and lampposts. Decorated trees were in shop windows, illuminating the night. Fashion Flare had a tree in the window, coordinating the colors with the garments on display.

Ray turned to Bonnie as they studied the tree in the Elements window. "You don't have a Christmas tree," he commented.

She shook her head. "I'm so busy and all, I don't bother. I mean, after all, I've got the one at the B & B and we have one for mom at her house." She lifted her shoulders in a shrug and moved on toward the Shoppe.

"Close the door and lock it," Dorian said as they stepped into the Shoppe. Even the Shoppe had a beautiful tree standing in the corner, its tiny lights twinkling in the darkened front.

They moved to the kitchen, where Morgan and Dorian were moving around, stirring a large pot and getting bowls. "Just in time," Dorian said. "Morgan fixed her mom's lima bean and ham soup. Even better than Sim's."

"Yum," Bonnie said and looked at Ray. "You are in for a treat."

Dorian handed Ray a couple of bowls filled with soup. "Distribute and grab a seat," he said, giving Bonnie a plate piled with cornbread scones.

She took her place beside Eryk and patted the chair next to her. Ray nodded and put a bowl of soup in front of her and one in front of Jenn, turning back for more. Dorian handed off two more, and Ray set them in front of John and Sim.

"Sit," Morgan said. "We're done." She took a seat next to Sim and smiled. "Eat up. It's best while it's piping hot." She grabbed some cornbread and passed it around.

Ray took a taste and grinned. "This is terrific. I wasn't sure how I'd feel about a soup made from lima beans. Never had it. This is phenomenal."

"Do you have any family favorites?" Bonnie asked.

"Probably the District Chophouse and Brewery," he said, buttering a piece of cornbread. "Mom's not much of a cook. Neither is dad. I kinda take after them."

"Oh." Bonnie couldn't imagine. So much of Ruthorford's social life revolved around either the B & B dining room or the Tea Room. Then, there were the sisters and their pies. She smiled at Ray. "It's okay. You're here now. We'll feed you."

Jenn laughed. "And you'll gain about twenty pounds if you aren't careful. Descendants' metabolisms run really high. Us non-descendants have to be very careful."

John leaned over. "I happen to love your curves," he said, not as quietly as he'd wished, garnering a poke from Sim, who sat on his other side.

Sim looked up and started signing to Ray, *They filled me in. Thank you for helping us.*

Eryk translated.

"My pleasure," he said as he felt Bonnie's leg press into his at the table. "I really do need to learn sign language."

Bonnie can teach you. My aunts taught her while I was learning. Sim directed his look at Bonnie as he signed and Eryk spoke.

They filled Ray in on the holiday activities, with the carol walk, the kids' Santa breakfast, and the huge Christmas Eve dinner, followed by a midnight service at the Chapel. Then, there were drop-in parties at Ozzy's and Sandra's and Eryk and Jasmine's. Not to forget the holiday shopping blitz coming up. Kids got to go shopping in groups, and the stores put things on credit so the parents wouldn't know until after Christmas. So far, no one had bought a Maserati, much to Dorian's dismay. He kept hinting to his twins.

After the table was cleared, Ray showed them the drawing he and Bonnie had produced. Jenn set the library sketches next to it. They really didn't match what he'd drawn. Then she pulled another drawing from her case, sitting it on the table.

"Where did you get that?" Dorian asked. He'd never seen it before, and it looked similar to what Ray had drawn.

"Meadow sent it to me. After I told her what was happening, she pulled a couple of those trunks from storage and started going through them. Remember that book we found in the case in the cave?" Jenn asked.

Ray knew he'd heard the name but wasn't sure where.

"She's my cousin," John said. "Her mother is Native American, and her father, who is deceased, was from Scotland. She inherited his Keep."

"Like in castle?" Ray asked.

"Pretty much," Jenn supplied. "Anyway, she found another leather-bound book with some markings she couldn't make out and a few drawings. This was one of them. Based on what I told her, she thinks this might fit."

Seeing Ray's look, Jenn pulled out another picture. It was a sketch of a man standing next to what appeared to be a dragon.

Ray studied it. "You're joking, right?" He then looked at the people sitting around him and said, "Never mind," which got some chuckles from around the table.

"Trust me, this doesn't particularly make us feel copacetic. Hasn't since we saw that first picture," Morgan said.

"So, you're telling me there's a cave in Scotland, in a castle, big enough for a dragon to come through. And who's the guy?" Ray pulled the drawing closer to study it, looking from the original Gulatega, his, then the larger one. "You know, it wouldn't take too far a stretch of the imagination," he looked up, "and since I have been asked to stretch my imagination since early today, for me to see this as a juvenile form of the large one. Or…maybe there are two different ones. I guess we can't ask this guy, can we?"

Sim signed, a huge grin on his face, *We haven't figured out time travel—at least not yet.* This time it was Bonnie who translated.

"Too bad," Ray commented.

"That picture is centuries old," Jenn explained.

"Why don't we go out to the cottage and give Ray a demonstration." Morgan stood.

He followed them out the back door. In front of him lay two large gardens, with a path between them, leading to a single-story cottage with a high-peaked roof. In the dimness, he saw what appeared to be high brick walls along the sides and the back. Light from the cottage shone through diamond-shaped windows over the garden and, from a side window, over a gazebo, which sat under a large tree. A Christmas tree's lights twinkled in the middle of the cottage's wide window.

He leaned over to Bonnie. "Even the cottage has a Christmas tree," he murmured, teasing her.

Dorian held the Dutch-door open and they stepped inside. As Dorian moved past, Ray looked about the cottage. Facing them along the far wall was a large fireplace, in front of which sat a long sofa. Along the wall opposite the fireplace was a long bank of cabinets making up a single-line kitchen. The room was wide enough to allow plenty of space behind the sofa and the kitchen for it not to feel cramped. Large windows with diamond-shaped panes filled the left end of the cottage, facing the back of the Shoppe. In front of the windows stood a Christmas tree. At the opposite end of the room from the windows were French doors, through which he could see a pretty Victorian bed.

As an artist, he loved the soft use of color, giving it a welcoming, warm feeling. "It's lovely," he said and started to close the Dutch door.

"Leave that open," Dorian said. "If, by some chance, we can attract it and it can go through, so much the better."

Ray frowned but did as he was told and walked over to the tree, taking Bonnie's hand. He wasn't sure why, but he felt a sudden sense of unease. He felt his heart rate go down and looked over at Bonnie and grinned.

An oval braided rug lay in front of the French doors. Morgan and Dorian stood in the center of the rug, joining hands. He was too far away to be sure, but he would have put money on their eyes taking on a swirling motion. Slowly, stones on the mantle and around the room, which he hadn't even noticed, began to emit a soft glow. As they became brighter, he could hear a hum. He saw a spark seem to rise from the rug, upward, between the pair. He closed his eyes, concentrating, and opened them. Everything in the room took on sharper colors, and the sparks turned into a multicolored iridescent fire. He heard Bonnie's intake of breath and tightened his hold on her hand.

He glanced around the room but saw no movement. Now, knowing what to look for, he looked at the door. Nothing.

"Anything?" John, who'd been watching him, asked.

"No," Ray said.

Morgan's hair flared out in its own red flame as the iridescent fire burst higher and then disappeared in a flash. Morgan's hair fell back into place and Dorian stepped forward, taking her into his arms. She laid her head against his shoulder and closed her eyes.

Ray closed his eyes again and opened them, returning his vision to normal. He glanced at Bonnie and saw her eyes looked normal, as well. He felt like, at this point, he was stabilizing Bonnie. He liked the feeling that he could help her for a change.

"Other than that freaky fire coming from the rug, the stones glowing, and that humming, it's a pretty awesome place."

"You're welcome to stay here," Morgan offered with a smile.

He couldn't tell if she was joking or not. "Thanks, but I like being closer to someone else making me food."

"Good save," John said.

With Dorian's arm still around Morgan, Dorian nodded toward the bedroom. "Eryk and Jasmine stay here some. So do Morgan's adoptive parents. No problem. What is important is you saw what it took to open that tiny portal. The one in the cemetery is about five times that size and neither Morgan and I nor Jasmine and Eryk have been able to open it. It literally knocks us on our butts."

"Then how do you know how big it is?"

Ignoring the question, Morgan said, "Let's head back to the house and I'll make us something to drink. Coffee, tea, soda, wine. This is a little rough on me, has been since I had the twins."

"Another reason to let Eryk and Sim try," Dorian said. "I don't want something that size hitting her full force."

As they left, Ray looked at the back of the Shoppe. It stood three stories and had windows and gables all aglow with candlelight in the windows. The light from the kitchen bid them welcome.

They all piled around the table and, before long, had mugs and glasses in front of them. Bonnie had been quiet, even for her. He looked at her and knew her mind was working.

"Just what do you want Ray to do?" she asked.

Sim nodded to Eryk. Obviously, they'd discussed this at length. Eryk spoke. "Since Ray seems to attract it, we figured he can be around town, and when it next shows up, he can text us and we'll go with him to the cemetery, hoping that thing will follow. Once we're there, we're going to put him up in the tree behind where it opens—and away from the creature—and, hopefully, open the portal, sending it back through."

"What if it doesn't want to go?" Bonnie asked.

Morgan spoke. "One thing about those creatures, at least the Gulatega, they can't seem to resist an open portal. We never have to chase them. Once it's open, they are attracted to it and go through it. Since I've been here, we hear when they are about, usually from the owls taking flight. Usually, a parliament."

"Parliament?"

"That's the word for the whole flock."

Sim signed. *Don't worry. My aunts will educate you on everything owls, given half a chance.*

Bonnie laughed as she interpreted. "And they will. As a little girl, I found myself cleaning the barn while they taught me to sign." She saw Ray's frown and answered. "The owls roost in their barn."

"Speaking of owls," Ray spoke up, "what's going to keep Oho from chasing it away?"

On my way to join you, I'm going to secure Oho so he won't. He won't like it, but I don't have a choice. If he stays, the others won't go, either. This time, Eryk spoke for Sim, almost at the same time as Sim was speaking. Ray noticed a look pass between them but said nothing.

"Why do you think Ray will be safe in the tree?" Bonnie asked.

"We've never seen them off the ground," Dorian answered, not with Morgan nor Mel, the GateKeeper before her. I was her ward," he explained.

Ray started to speak, but Bonnie interrupted him, "We've never had one with wings before, either."

"From what I saw and the pictures we put together, I think those aren't developed. At least I hope they aren't," Ray said as much to Bonnie as the others. "But I do have a question. Where do they go? Any ideas."

Eryk looked at Dorian, then at Jenn, who nodded.

Dorian spoke. "This is speculation but also from a little evidence. We think there's another world on another plane. You've heard us talk about Meadow. Her father was Ian. We don't know if he'd been affected by the creatures or was crazy in his own right, but he'd created a lab of some sort in a castle he built in Virginia Beach."

Ray's eyes widened. "I know that place. Not that I've ever been inside, but it's quite famous."

"Well, he hired a guy to help him artificially open a portal. We don't know if it was there or if he caused it. He kidnapped Morgan to get us to open it, so he could go through, declaring he was more like the creatures than descendants. It was obvious he was dying. There was a group of Gulatega that stayed around him. We got it open, and they carried him through. That portal was huge. Oh, and that information falls into the 'secret' part of the NDA."

"Is the portal still there?" Ray asked, adding a nod in confirmation of what they'd told him. Who'd believe him anyway?

"It seemed to be deactivated when they went through. But we took all the stones, removed all the lab notes, and did everything we could think of to neutralize it."

Bonnie's eyes got big. She hadn't heard the whole story. "What guarantees are there that it won't pull Ray through with it?"

Sim looked at Eryk, who spoke. "Well, we had planned to secure Ray to the tree before we opened the portal."

"Don't tell me anymore. I'm no hero. Let's just do this. Sooner rather than later," Ray said.

Bonnie's voice sank into Sim's brain, a silent demand. *"You damned well better bring him back to me."*

Sim looked at her and sent her warmth as his voice filled her mind, *"I will do my damnedest. Besides, I like him."*

Her unexpected chuckle had Ray looking at her. She covered with, "I was just thinking of what outsiders would think if they could hear this conversation."

"Good save, squirt." Sim's words held a mental caress.

"So, all I have to do is act normal until it shows."

"That's it."

"Well, I'm done for tonight," Bonnie said. "Ray, you can walk me home if you're through. If not, I'll see myself home." There was no stopping them. Even knowing it was necessary, she didn't like it one bit.

He debated for just a second. As long as she didn't touch him, she wouldn't feel his heart rate and know he was scared shitless. Then, he looked into her eyes and knew he wanted to be with her more than he wanted to save face.

Chapter Twenty

Stepping outside, they stopped on the stoop in front of the Shoppe. The wind had picked up, sending a chill through them both. Their heads turned toward the sisters' house, half anticipating the screech of an owl. Only silence surrounded them. She stepped down and jogged toward the median, taking the shortcut to the other side and kept going, heading around the building toward her apartment.

Ray raced to catch up, staying silent as she ran up the stairs to her apartment. As always, it remained unlocked, something that no longer astonished him since he knew about the descendants. No one with any brains would threaten them. Except, no one knew they were descendants. He shook the thought out of his head as he followed her inside.

He'd barely gotten the door closed when she turned to him, putting her arms around his waist.

"Kiss me," she whispered. "Please kiss me."

He was more than willing to comply, capturing her cold lips with his. In mere seconds, their lips warmed and she opened, inviting him into her intimacy.

When he could barely contain himself, he pulled himself back. Taking a deep breath, he whispered, "Isn't this where you tell me you have to go help someone close?"

"No. This is where I ask you to stay with me tonight."

His heart stilled. He looked at her. Yes, he saw desire, but he also saw fear. "You know that there's nothing I want more than to be with you. But not like this. Not because you are afraid of what could happen." He pulled her close, holding her.

"But," she started, leaning against his chest, but she couldn't finish before the tears started.

"I know," he said. "I'm not going to lie. I'm scared, too."

"Will you at least stay? We don't have to do anything."

"Bonnie, I don't know that I could do that. You are way too tempting. Not tonight. Let's let this sink in for both of us. Let's get over the fear first."

He moved back, lifting her chin, making her look at him. "Let's do this right."

She nodded. "Then, I guess I better go help Sandra close."

"That's my girl. Hey, do you think you could steal some pie for us?"

She grinned at him. "I can almost guarantee it. I'll text you when we're done."

They headed back, holding hands. When they got to the lobby, he leaned and kissed her, then watched her disappear into the dining room before heading to his room.

He pulled out his phone. He'd put it on silent earlier and had missed two calls from his parents, one from his mom and one from his dad. He hit speed dial.

"Hey guys, I put it on silent and forgot. Everything okay?"

"Yes. How are you? You called from the hospital, and then we didn't hear anything. We sent messages but didn't hear back. If we'd known where you were, we'd have come," his mother said.

"I'm fine. They not only fixed the clot, but they also managed to return the use of my hand. I've been painting. Not the best cell service here."

"Son, that's wonderful," his father said. "About the hand, I mean. Not the cell service. We've decided to go up to the Catskills this year. Wish you could go with us."

"I got to meet KC. She's given me a space to work in the art gallery she runs. I think I'll stay here and give my fingers some practice. I've got an art therapist, but it's going to take a lot of work on my part."

"KC? The KC?"

"Yeah. She's super nice. Married to a local guy. I hope you two have a wonderful Christmas. Hey, mom, dad, I love you."

"We love you, too. Happy holidays."

"I'll call you after the holidays. We'll get together then."

"That would be great. Talk to you then."

He hung up and hit another number. "Hi. Are you busy? Great. I'll be right up."

With a grin on his face, he left the room.

***

The dining room was buzzing with activity. Teresa had gone up to put Aby down and Bonnie wanted a moment to talk with Sandra, someone her own age.

"You mean he turned you down?" Sandra said.

Bonnie glanced around. "Shhh, I don't want anyone, especially Teresa, to hear. Then, he said he wanted to have pie with me after I finish cleaning."

"And he is attracted to you?" Bonnie tried to put it delicately.

"Oh, yeah. There's no doubt about that. I just don't know what to do. Part of me wants to run home and hide and the other part wants to see this play out. I really, really like him."

Sandra walked over and put her hands on Bonnie's shoulders. "You know, he's probably going to leave and go back to his life soon."

Bonnie nodded. "I just never felt this way about anyone and, if I'm going to experience...." She let the words die off.

Sandra's eyes narrowed. "Experience what exactly?" She threw up her hands. "Oh my God. You're a virgin!"

"Shhh." Bonnie put her hand over Sandra's mouth. "And now all of Ruthorford knows it."

Sandra stepped around Bonnie and peeked through the glass. Everyone was involved in their own conversations. When she turned back, she said in a high whisper, "How is this even possible. I mean. What about Clay?"

Bonnie shrugged and started wiping down the counter. Sandra put her hand over Bonnie's. "I swear, girl, you are going to wipe a hole in that spot. What happened with Clay? I figured you two had broken up because I haven't seen much of him since he went to work at the horse farm."

"Honestly, I felt like he was doing all the wanting and trying to drag me along. I just didn't feel it. I wasn't sure what *it* was, but now I'm sure. I do feel it with Ray. Boy, do I ever feel it. Sadly, he doesn't want me."

"Whoa. From the way I've seen him look at you like you're fresh cream and he's a starved tiger, I'd say those feelings are mutual. It's got to be something else. Hey, maybe he's an honorable man."

Bonnie leaned back against the counter. "Just my luck."

Sandra couldn't help but laugh. "So, don't go running away from this. He's got his reasons. Respect that. Don't go playing a Clay on him. You fix the best pie we've got and take it to him." She held up her hand when Bonnie's eyes widened. "Don't jump him. Have pie with him. Maybe he'll open up about what's causing his hesitation."

"Well, he did mention not wanting us to do anything with what's pending with the creature."

"See. Morgan told me some of it. I think he's damned brave to offer himself up as bait." When she saw the anxiety in Bonnie's eyes, she rushed on. "You know damned well Eryk and Sim won't let anything happen to him."

"They'll try. I've just got a bad feeling about this."

"Like what? Have you told Sim?"

"Nothing concrete. He'll just think I'm being a scaredy cat. He always says that because I didn't take the chances he wanted me to growing up."

"Never have figured you two out. You all seemed joined at the hip. Not Claire so much. But you. I really thought you and he would get together one day."

"Eww! He's like a brother. Always has been." She smiled, thinking back. "Okay, not when I was too young to know better. Then, he was my Prince Charming. I adored him. He outgrew me, moving on to girls with boobs. He made sure the sibling relationship we'd had remained and grew stronger. He feels like my brother. An annoying as hell brother, but a brother I adore and would defend to the death, nevertheless."

Sandra glanced through the diamond window of the door once more. "Speaking of which, he and Di are heading this way. You pull him aside and tell him about your concerns." She said and then laughed. "Not about your feelings about Ray. Hell, he'd kill the man himself. About your worries about what they are planning."

Sandra shut up as the two walked into the kitchen, one toting pies and the other a basket with boxes of pastries. Lots of pastries. Di spoke, laughing. "You know how he is when he's concentrating," she set the pastries on the counter. "And the pies are from his aunts."

Sim was watching Bonnie, who kept looking at the floor. He walked over and took her hand, pulling her through the kitchen door.

When Di turned, Sandra stopped her. "Let them go have a chat. She's worried about Ray. I want her to tell Sim. Seems like he's already sensed it."

"He is remarkable that way." She glanced toward the door. "About some things." She patted her tummy. "About others, not so much."

"Di? Seriously?" Sandra squealed.

"Shh. You know he can hear everything. I didn't want to say anything until I was sure. Still a little early. And, with Morgan losing the baby, I...I don't know what to do."

"I do." She pulled Di into a hug. "We celebrate everything around here. What happened with Morgan was early and it was natural. It happens. She was sad but seems okay now. Truthfully, I don't think it was her first miscarriage. I'm sure they will try again. She's been very excited about my expanding waistline." She patted her own rounding stomach. "Seems we're gonna fill up Ruthorford with new descendants, one way or another. Well, you better tell him and soon," Sandra said right before Sim and Bonnie walked back in.

He looked from one to the other but didn't sign.

"We better get back. He left the kitchen in a mess."

Did not, Sim signed.

"Did, too," Di said and pushed through the swinging kitchen door.

Sandra looked at Bonnie. "Did you tell him?"

Bonnie just nodded.

"Well, put together a tray with this still-hot pie on it, heavy on the whipped cream, and take it down the hall. Nothing makes a man chatty like the sisters' pie."

Nerves still taut, Bonnie knocked lightly on the door.

"Come in. It's not locked," Ray called out. As she entered, he stood, closing the sketchbook. "I thought you were going to text me?"

She stopped. "I can take this back," she offered.

"Oh, no, you don't," he said and rushed forward, taking the tray from her hands. "Do you know how good this pie smells?"

"Oh yeah. Sim and Di just delivered them from the sisters. I wanted you to have it while it was still warm. I also brought a carafe of coffee, the one you like so much."

"I don't care what you want, but the answer is yes." He laughed and set the plates, mugs, and carafe on the table."

Bonnie raised a brow, teasing him.

"That's even negotiable, depending on how good the pie is," he teased back.

Suddenly, she felt better, comfortable with him, like they had been. She plopped down in the chair, cut off a bite of pie, raised it to her mouth, and looked at him. "Naw, I've changed my mind. I don't think I want you to be my first."

Ray choked on the pie he was trying to swallow. "What?"

"I said—"

He pointed at her with his fork. "I know what you said. I just want to know when you were planning on telling me this little bit of information. In my book, it's kinda important."

"Why?"

He floundered. "Well…it just is." He caught his footing and went on. "First of all, it's harder for the woman the first time, and a man needs to be more careful."

Bonnie put her elbow on the table and leaned her chin into the palm of her hand. "Go on."

"Stop it, Bonnie. You know the facts of life. I would just like to have been made aware of this. It's got to be a pretty important decision for you if you've waited this long."

She sat back and picked up her fork again, cutting into the pie. "It is. I realized a long time ago that it was about as intimate as one could get, and I wasn't willing to share that with just anyone. As to the hymen, I don't have one," she added casually.

Ray choked again. "God, Bonnie. I'm going to die eating this damned pie. Can we talk about something else?" he begged.

"So, are you prepared to live in an alternate universe if you get sucked through the portal?" she asked casually, taking a sip of coffee to wash down the pie.

"Geesh, Bonnie, are you sure you aren't Claire, sent in Bonnie's place to just torture me?" Of course, he knew she wasn't. The eyes and that voice. And, inside, he was loving that she was teasing him. Still uncomfortable, but enjoying it nevertheless.

"Oh, Claire's definitely not a virgin," she said casually.

This time, he just gulped down coffee. When he looked up, he saw the twinkle in her eyes and started laughing. Then, she joined him, and they continued laughing while they finished the pie. Bonnie turned the conversation to stories of Dorian and Eryk, telling him about them being separated at birth and finding one another when Jasmine saw Eryk doing his magician's act at the Virginia State Fair.

"Eryk? Wait. You mean that's Eryk Vreeland? God, why didn't I put that together?"

"Um-hm," she said, nodding. "I think you've been a little busy, don't you?" She sipped some coffee before continuing. "He and Jasmine fell in love while she was working at Safe Harbor in Virginia—Jenn's organization for housing and helping abused families, now being run by Kayla, John's cousin and Meadow's mom. They came back here, and he bought a rather derelict town a couple of miles away and set up shop for them and his troupe of performers."

"How could I not have known? I've seen him perform."

"Same way people don't always recognize you, although they've seen you at showings. Here, he's just Eryk, brother to Dorian and a descendant."

"Are his abilities more like Dorian's or Sim's," he asked. He'd wondered since the meeting since Eryk was taking Dorian's place.

"Definitely more like Sim's. No one here is like Sim. But no one is sure, either, because when the sisters found him on their porch as an infant and adopted him, they decided that his DNA would not be tested. And it never has been."

"I wonder why?"

"No one knows, and, with the sisters, their word is usually law. They've been here forever and...let's just say don't let their venerable age fool you."

"Well, they certainly have a way about them."

"I adore them. But I also wouldn't cross them." She stood. "I really do need to go close. I am sending Sandra home since Ozzy's getting in tonight."

Ray stood as well, taking the plate out of her hand and setting it down, pulling her to him. "Don't, for one moment, think that because I am being cautious, I don't want you, my Bonnie lassie." With that, he yanked her to him and took her mouth with his, letting his desire show.

As he pulled her tight against his body, her arms went around his neck, and she gave back with the same power he was giving her. She felt his erection against her stomach and felt her own insides respond, matching passion for passion.

When he stepped back, they were both breathing heavily, and their hearts were pounding in unison. "I want you more than I've ever wanted anyone, ever. And, I will have you—when the time is right."

He loaded the tray and carried it to the door. "I'd walk you back, but I'm afraid my desire would be on display for everyone."

Glancing down, she nodded and smiled. "Thank you."

"Oh, yeah. Any time."

Chapter Twenty-One

The next couple of days passed quickly, with Ray joining in the festivities, standing with Bonnie as they sang carols, sneaking out to do some shopping, and being available for the children as they were turned loose to shop. He'd never seen anything like it. Kids ran from store to store, talking to anyone who wasn't their parents, getting ideas. He found he'd toted more bags with names on them to the B & B than he'd thought possible. Turned out, Teresa stored them in the parlor and then held a gift-wrapping marathon for the kids, with some adults supervising and helping. He was immediately recruited. With each event, he fell more and more in love with Ruthorford, to the point of forgetting why he was constantly running around the town in the first place.

And, so far, no sign of the creature. He was truly grateful it hadn't occurred when the children had been running around. With his wrapping shift late afternoon, he found he had part of the morning to take care of what he'd been planning and got finished just before he was to report to the dining room.

The kids had had snacks while Eryk and Jasmine performed a magic act, which he'd thoroughly enjoyed himself, when Teresa stepped in and sent the kids from the earlier shift home and began setting up the tables for the next wrapping extravaganza.

By the time the children were done and gone, and the adults had finished dinner, Ray was whipped. He helped bus tables and finish closing so he could walk Bonnie home. Of course, their good night kisses were getting longer and more intense, making him wonder how much longer he could keep his hands off her luscious body.

Bonnie walked out of the kitchen. "Oh, Ray, you don't have to walk me home. I know you've got to be as beat as I am. What a day! But those smiling faces made it all worthwhile."

"Nope. Not going to happen. Besides, I don't care how tired I am, I am not going to miss kissing you goodnight."

Just that statement made her stomach flutter. She took his extended hand and they stepped out into the night, scanning the street for almost invisible movement. Nothing. They walked and stopped again in the alleyway, just as they'd done every night since the meeting at the Shoppe, waiting. Again, nothing. He even got in a couple of stolen kisses before they headed to the apartment.

"You don't have to come in," she began.

"Unless you are telling me no, I'm coming in."

She chuckled and opened the door, her voice becoming quiet as she stepped in the hallway.

"Oh, Ray," she whispered, tears forming. In front of her, in front of the window, stood a Christmas tree, fully decorated. "When did you do this?" she asked over her shoulder as she moved forward until she stood in front of the tree.

"This morning, while you were working."

She reached out and touched one of several small snowy owls placed among red ribbons and ornaments. "Where did you get the ornaments?"

"Teresa helped me. She had some old boxes of ornaments she let me go through. I hope it's okay. It was so much fun. I've never decorated a tree before."

She turned to him. "Never?"

He shook his head.

"It's perfect," she said and moved into his arms. "No one has ever given me a more perfect gift." With that, she turned her lips up to his.

He took her mouth, soft and pliant, there in the room lit only by the twinkle of tiny lights and felt his heart take the rhythm of hers.

She finally pulled back. "As much as I would love to beg you to stay, I have to be up early in the morning. I'm covering for Sandra."

He stepped back. "And to think, tonight you just might have gotten lucky," he teased.

"Don't even." She pushed him toward the door, laughing. "Sleep in tomorrow. You've earned it."

He stopped at the door. "You know, I can't remember when I've had a better day."

Bonnie reached over and pulled a piece of tape off of his sweater. "Or a noisier one," she added and held up the tape.

He kissed her on the nose. "Got get some sleep. Dream of me."

"I will. I always do." She closed the door and leaned against it, looking at the Christmas tree glowing in the dark. Smiling, she went to the bedroom, changed into her pj's, grabbed a pillow and the blanket, and went back and lay down on the couch, wanting to sleep by her tree.

As had become his habit, Ray walked down the street, passed the boutique and the empty shops next to it, by the old sisters' house, crossing in front of Ozzy and Sandra's place, and heading back up the other side. It was by the alley across from the sisters' house, near Elements, that he felt the tingle, sending goosebumps through him. He reached into his pocket, pulled out his phone, and hit one number and then another, immediately sending the instant messages that had been set up.

He was afraid to move, afraid he'd lose it. He closed his eyes, concentrated, and opened them, looking down. About a foot away from his feet, he saw the outline of what appeared to be a tail. "Shit," he mumbled and heard the door to the Shoppe open.

"Walk toward me, slowly," Eryk said. "Sim's on his way."

"Okay." His voice came out with a slight quiver. He began walking.

"I'm right behind you." A voice settled in his head. *"It's Sim. Keep walking. Head to the cemetery. Eryk will fall in next to me."*

"Did you think now was the perfect time to show me you can do this?" Ray asked. "It could have saved me from having to learn all that damned sign language."

A warm chuckle filled his mind.

"Is Eryk in there, too?"

"No. I can't do it. It's just you and Sim. Oh, you can answer him mentally, as well." Eryk's laughter came from behind him.

"Good," Ray said out loud. *"Fuck you,"* he sent the message to Sim as they walked past the post office.

Again, laughter, much louder, filled his mind.

Aloud, he asked, "Is it still here. I'm not feeling it."

Eryk spoke, "Sim says it's a bit to the left and ahead of you like it's leading you to the cemetery."

"Oh, this is just great." Ray felt the palms of his hands start to sweat and put his phone away.

"You'll have to adjust your own heart rate. I'm not bringing Bonnie into this," Sim's words slipped into Ray's mind.

"Good thing or I'd have to kill you after this is over." Ray thought back.

"You remember what we discussed?" Eryk asked.

"Yeah, climb the fucking tree and pray that thing can't climb or fly—yet," Ray said. "Speaking of which, is Oho safe and secure?"

The answering voice in his head was warmer. *"He is. Thanks."*

"Good thing I have great night vision. It's pitch black out here." He kept walking.

They were almost to the cemetery and his heart felt like a hammer. He concentrated, remembering how it felt when Bonnie eased the rhythm, and he felt his heart slow.

"Good job," Sim thought.

"Just shut up," Ray said out loud. "You two get that portal opened and shove that son-of-a-bitch through. My legs are feeling wobbly."

They approached the tree. Sim hopped up on the first limb like it was a small step instead of four feet off the ground, held out his hand, grabbed Ray's, and pulled him up with little effort. Once he was on the limb, Sim put a chain around Ray's waist, closing the heavy-duty spring snap.

"Is this really necessary?" Ray asked, now snug against the body of the tree.

"We don't want you accidentally pulled into that portal. We have no idea what it would do."

"Oh great. Just great. Can you see it? I can't."

"Yeah, it's on its hind legs against the tree, looking at you." Sim put the words into both Ray's and Eryk's minds. With that, Sim hopped down away from the tree and joined Eryk in front.

Ray closed his eyes, concentrated, and opened them. The world took on a mosaic effect, colors flashing.

Eryk and Sim clasped wrists, figuring it would be a stronger hold and they might not be thrown apart. Both closed their eyes and concentrated. When they opened their eyes, the irises swirled, and their eyes began to glow.

Ray noticed stones on the ground started to glow and wondered if they'd placed them there or if they'd always been there. A hum resonated and grew louder. A vibration, subtle at first, then intensifying, ran through the tree and into his body.

His enhanced vision picked up shimmering sparks as they shot up from the ground. The creature danced back, apparently agitated. Sim and Eryk moved back a step to where the sparks were no longer under them but between them and the tree.

Ray gripped the limb above him tighter as the opening expanded and his friends' eyes glowed in a more violet light, similar to the creatures. His palms grew damp and his heart raced.

His feet felt like they were on fire as energy pulled at him, and Ray was glad for the damned chain.

When the sparks turned to iridescent flames and reached higher, an outline of a man appeared in the flames, as much energy as the flames. The man's hand extended, made a motion, and the creature leaped past him through the portal.

Ray took a deep breath, no longer feeling the sting the animal had created. He felt something else. Images were shooting through his mind. He felt his consciousness being pushed down. He fought to remain on top. More images, things he didn't understand, flooded his mind like giant waves, forcing him under. He felt like he was losing consciousness.

"Why did you chain him?" It was more image than words, but he seemed to understand.

"To protect him from your creature." He recognized Sim's voice in his head, growing stronger, fighting the other. Shit. It sure was getting crowded in here. He tried to respond. He was either ignored, or they couldn't hear him. He didn't have control. He couldn't force either out.

"He is one of the last of his kind. I will close this opening now."

Images, brighter than any colors Ray had ever seen, flashed in lightning speed through his mind. He felt Sim's words. *"Why not me? Why him or through him?"*

"You have a natural barrier. All of our progeny do. This one is open. You will learn from his images. I cannot stay on your plane. I will not harm him. Your mind will absorb from him. You have done well."

"Ian?" Sim forced the thought as fast as possible as he felt the connection weaken.

"Your kind cannot survive on the other side and neither can mine on this. Well, almost." The entity's attention was drawn past Sim.

"What in the hell have you done?" Grace's voice came as a roar as she and Alice raced forward toward Eryk and Sim.

The entity bowed his head toward the two women and stepped back. With a sudden flash and a loud crack, the portal closed. Ray felt a searing pain and fell forward, landing on the spot where the portal had been. Eryk and Sim's connection broke, and they were tossed to the side with such force it knocked the wind out of Eryk.

"Is he dead?" Eryk asked, crawling toward Ray.

"Not by any thanks to you. You idiots," Alice's voice no longer had that sing-song she normally portrayed. It resonated and vibrated through his brain, similar to what Ray had heard in his head from the man. He fought to pull his mind back to consciousness, slipping up and down as if on a moss-covered wall.

Eryk joined the sisters who were kneeling beside Ray now. The sisters placed their hands on Ray's head and pushed energy into his mind.

Lights burst around him. "Shit! Damn!" he screamed and moaned at the pain his own words brought.

"Good. Let's get him back. Take him to our house so we can care for him," Grace said, rising with the agility of a teenager.

"His body's smoking!" Eryk shouted.

"Oh, for heaven's sake," Alice said and leaned over, putting her hand over Ray's stomach. "There."

As Eryk and Sim put their hands under his arms to raise him, Ray looked back at the tree. It stood tall and straight, with none of the damage he would have suspected. The chain, however, was broken in the middle, the ends melted, dangling from the tree. He looked down at his middle where a slight iridescence glowed. He closed his eyes, and when he opened them, the dark of the night surrounded him.

"I can walk," Ray protested.

"Shut up. Let them help you, or I'll have Sim carry you," Grace said as the two sisters led the way, walking taller and straighter than Ray had ever seen them.

Ray glanced from Sim to Eryk. Eryk just shook his head and mumbled, "Don't ask. We're in enough trouble as it is."

Struggling to remain alert, Ray thought back, searching for something. He wasn't sure what. The last thing he remembered was watching Eryk and Sim clasp hands, then this excruciating pain in his head. Giving up, he finally asked, "Did it work?"

Sim nodded.

"Good," Ray said and passed out as they crossed the median to the old sisters' place. Sim scooped him up and jogged up the steps, following Grace and Alice into the house.

Soon after they got him on the bed upstairs, Teresa arrived. When she stepped into the room, she saw Ray passed out on the bed, Eryk and Sim standing on one side, and the sisters on the other.

"What happened?"

Alice turned to her and glared. "I can't believe you were a part of this."

Teresa smiled at her, not quelled by the tone. "You were aware of what was going on. Don't play innocent with me," she retorted.

Alice appeared to huff when Grace narrowed her eyes at her sister. "No matter. You are the keeper of memories. We need your assistance."

"So are you," Teresa responded.

"I want you to do it. I don't want this information in just my or Sim's hands."

Teresa looked at Sim, who nodded. The sisters stepped back, giving Teresa room. She stepped over to the bed and laid her hand on his forehead. "He's clammy," she said. "Is he all right?"

"He will be. Proceed."

She placed one hand on his arm, reached up, and placed the other on his neck, cupping the back of it.

"You might want to sit down," Grace suggested.

Teresa sat on the edge of the bed and took a deep breath, closed her eyes, and let the information flow from him to her.

Eryk stared. It was the longest he had ever seen Teresa hold contact with someone she was reading. He watched her face as it flushed, then grew pale. He started to step forward when Alice held up her hand, stopping him.

After a while, Teresa pulled her hands back and stood.

Eryk saw the slight trembling in her hands before she clasped them together.

She looked from the two men to the sisters, letting her hands fall to her sides, standing tall. "He's an innocent. Make him well." It was an order.

Grace stopped her before she left the room. "Do you want him to remember?"

"I don't know. Let's get him on his feet for now. We can always open his memory." With that, she left the room without looking back.

Bonnie sat straight up, listening. A soft knock sounded on her door. She blinked. The tree glowed in the front window in the dark. She rubbed her eyes. "Coming," she said and walked over to the door, pulling it open. Seeing Teresa, she stepped back. "It's Ray, isn't it?"

Teresa nodded. "It's not as bad as you're thinking. The creature came after he left you. Eryk and Sim, with Ray's help, managed to open the portal. But it didn't go as planned."

She followed Bonnie into the room and saw the tree, remembering Ray's excitement. "Nice tree," Teresa said.

"Thanks. Ray said you helped."

"I just pointed to boxes."

"How bad is it?"

"I think he'll be okay, but the old sisters intervened. He's at their house, unconscious. He won't remember—for now. I want you to go and be there when he wakes up. Keep his rhythm steady. They don't want him at the clinic. The sisters and Sim can handle him better right now."

"Do I want to know?"

"It doesn't matter right now. Let's get him stable."

Knowing better than to question Teresa's judgment, Bonnie nodded and went to change out of her pj's.

Chapter Twenty-Two

Ray woke to see his beautiful Bonnie sitting on the edge of the bed beside him. He tried to smile, but it made his hair hurt.

"Did I get drunk?" He looked around and saw he was in a bedroom, and his eyes widened. "Don't tell me we did the deed and I don't remember."

He heard a man chuckle from across the room and saw Eryk standing in the corner next to Sim, who was firing death threats with his eyes. At this point, death seemed like a better alternative than the pain in his head.

Bonnie laid her hand on his arm and matched his heart rate to hers. As she did, his headache receded a little.

Miss Alice stepped into the room, carrying a bed tray. "Good," her sweet voice carried, soothing his headache even more. "I have some of Sim's French onion soup for you. Added a cheese baguette on top, added cheese, and stuck it under the broiler. Heaven in a bowl. This will fix you right up."

"I can get up." He tried to push himself up and found he didn't have the strength to do much more than attain a sitting position.

Miss Alice set the tray over him, the deep bowl not sloshing a bit. She looked at the men. "Boys, yours is downstairs. I'll let our lassie Bonnie sit with him while he eats." Her next words were directed at him. "If you eat it all up, I have some fresh pie waiting for you."

Ray's mind flashed back to the ones Bonnie and he had shared not too long ago and he knew, by her blush, that she was remembering the same thing.

"I'll be right downstairs if you need anything. You did great, by the way. Thank you." With that, she turned and toddled out, following Sim and Eryk down the stairs.

"Eat," was all Bonnie said, watching him.

He took a bit, then another. Suddenly, he was starving. He'd finished half the bowl before he stopped. What was it about Ruthorford food? He made himself put down the spoon.

"I still have this headache, and I don't remember much. Okay, the last thing I remember was being in the tree, chained, I suppose, to hold me there, the creature trying to get to me and Eryk and Sim clasping arms. Did it work?"

"From what I understand, it did. They brought you here—I guess because it's Sim's aunts. I was retrieved to help stabilize you." She felt his arm again. "You appear stable. Tell me what happened," she said quietly.

"I left you, took my walk, got to the alley across from the sisters, and felt the tingle. I sent the text to Sim and Eryk and waited. They came and followed me to the cemetery." He frowned. "I think it was leading me there. Anyway, Sim got me in the tree, and they clasped wrists. I remember their eyes doing that swirly thing, rocks glowing, and sparks— just like at the cottage, except a whole lot bigger. I guess it went through. It must have burst or something, knocking me out because when I came to, I was looking at you."

She felt his heart rate jump under her hand and steadied it again.

He looked down at her hand. "I admit, grown man that I am, I was scared shitless. I've never been so scared, and I'm not sure why."

"Big, not so hairy, monster?" Bonnie asked, trying to keep it light.

"Yeah, but there's something else. I just can't remember. I will, but not right now." He looked around the room. "As nice as they are, I think I'd like to go back to my room."

"I think that can be arranged," Bonnie said and stood, taking the tray. "I'll be right back."

"Great. Oh, and Bonnie," he waited for her to turn back, "tell Sim to stay out of my head."

It was a good thing she hadn't been touching him, or he would have felt her pulse jump. She nodded and headed downstairs.

***

Teresa sat with Mike, Dorian, and Morgan when Ray stepped up to the dining room doorway. She turned and saw the bag in his hand.

"I'm checking out," he said, turned, and walked over to the counter.

Bonnie had just pushed through the kitchen door when she heard his statement. She set down the tray and walked to the lobby. "No goodbye?"

He looked at her, emotions deep in his eyes. "I debated it. I didn't know what would be best. I want to call you. To explain, but not right now. I can't."

"Okay. You take care." She leaned up and placed a kiss on his cheek, turned, and walked back into the dining room, past Teresa, not meeting her eyes. She walked into the kitchen, and in a few seconds, Sandra walked out, picked up the tray, and delivered the food.

Teresa took her place behind the counter as he pulled out his wallet. "No charge," she said.

"No," he replied. "I pay my way."

"And you more than have. Ruthorford thanks you." She turned, walked back into the dining room, and back to the table without another word.

She waited until she knew he had pulled away and went into the kitchen. Sandra was chopping vegetables while Bonnie kneaded dough. Over and over, methodical, slow, never looking up. Teresa walked over and pulled her hands up, dusted with flour. "Come on. I'm taking you home."

She shook her head. "I'm fine."

"No, you're not. Neither are we. I'm taking you home."

This time she nodded.

***

The descendants sat around the kitchen table in The Shoppe of Spells, much like they'd done for any crisis.

"Do you think he remembered?" Morgan asked.

"I don't know. I didn't touch him," Teresa said.

"How could he just walk away?" Dorian asked, exasperated and feeling impotent. Dorian had seen Bonnie's face as Teresa walked her home. For two cents, he'd have gone after Ray, but Teresa put her foot down. They were to leave him alone.

Now, she looked at Dorian. "How could he?" Teresa repeated. "We used him. Plain and simple. Not only did we use him, but *they* also used him. Apparently, like they have done for centuries, possibly millennia. Can't say I blame him for hightailing it out of here. Hell, if I thought I could get away from what I know, I might do the same thing."

"We still don't know what you know," John said, looking at Sim, who shrugged.

"It's my place, or the sisters, who agree with me on this, to share information as needed." She looked around the grumbling table. "Honestly, as we assimilate all the images we've received through Ray, we are trying to compile the information that correlates to the images. Memories, both theirs and ours. Jumbled images over long, interspersed periods of time. We really are descendants, for better or worse. We have a legacy, whatever it is." She took a deep breath and looked around the table. Sadness and unity, and a need for understanding shown in their eyes. "For right now, here's what I can tell you."

Morgan slid a mug of coffee in front of her. She took a sip. "To begin with, the cemetery portal is closed. The creature, which, in fact, is a bigger version of the Gulatega, is back on the other side. In their world, or dimension, whatever you want to call it, they are an endangered species. Unfortunately, it seems to have happened when Ian went over. He carried something—maybe like a virus or bacteria, real or energy, I'm not clear on that—that almost wiped them out. They were, to them, like our elephants."

"Except they could fly," Eryk supplied.

"That's our supposition. I think, and that's my supposition, that they may be part of the reason we have stories of dragons. That, and the bones of dinosaurs. Except, and this is driving me to distraction, I would think they couldn't be seen in this dimension. Never mind, I tailspin every time I start thinking about it. Let me tell you the more important part, which may, in a way, weave back to seeing the Gulatega in this dimension. Remember, these are flashes of imagery. Again, I'm putting together suppositions." She looked around the table, realizing she definitely had their attention. "They, the beings, at some point, discovered they could come through to our dimension. But, the only way they could stay was to take on corporeal form. I don't know what form they are in their world. When they are here, they are energy. They discovered that they could slip their energy into one of our forms, and when they did that, they could stay."

"What happened to the people they used?" Jenn asked.

"I'm guessing again, given what I saw from what happened in the cemetery, that their energy pushed that person's personality or essence down."

"They take over? Like Body Snatchers?" Dorian asked.

Teresa winced, but couldn't help but smile at the reference to the old movie. "Sort of, but not exactly. They gave them better health, knowledge, and a longer life."

"But no essence of their own, no free will," Dorian's anger was apparent."

"Us? What about us?" Morgan interrupted. "How did we come about? We not inhabited by some alien, are we?" Morgan asked.

"No. When that enhanced body mated with a normal human—for a better word—the offspring was human but carried some of the enhancements of the entity."

"It is my understanding that they developed rules about who they chose." She shook her head. "I'm obviously not doing this well. "Please understand that I have centuries of imagery in my head. I might not get it all in the right order."

Morgan looked at Dorian, placing her hand over her husband's, sending a push of calm when she felt a slight shock from his heightened energy.

He looked at his wife and nodded, deliberating lowering his energy. He wove his fingers with hers and smiled.

"How do we get to the Scot and the Native American?" John asked.

"Enhanced humans came over and mated with Native Americans." Teresa stopped, shaking her head. "Let me step back a bit. If two combined humans, let's call them hybrids, mated, they produced a truly enhanced human." She glanced at Sim and waited. When he nodded, she smiled and looked around the table before speaking, "Like Sim and the sisters."

"What?" Eryk asked.

"The sisters are direct products of two hybrids, two combined humans. Hence their abilities, longevity, and such. We really don't know where Sim came from, but the sisters immediately recognized him being the product of hybrid mating. They believe that whoever put him on their porch knew they were also the product of hybrids."

Questions flew at Sim, who just shook his head and nodded to Teresa.

As the questions now flew at her, Teresa held up her hand. "Remember, I am trying to digest this myself. What I've gotten is a combination of what was put into Ray's subconscious, what Sim gained from the merger, and what Sim's been kind enough to share with me."

"The progeny of the hybrids brought with them enhancements which, when added to the Native American enhancements, via Tanis, their daughter of the mountain, who probably was a hybrid, produced the descendants. Anyway, as time went on, we, descendants, have continued to evolve ourselves, hence Eryk and Jasmine." She picked up her coffee cup and took a slow drink. None of this sat well with her, but it was what it was.

Sim signed to Teresa. She nodded.

"When they opened the portal, the entity—for a better term—came through. They apparently can't fuse or meld with a descendant. I don't know if that's by design or choice. But, there was Ray, all human. The entity melded with Ray so he could communicate, pulling Sim into Ray's mind, and pushing Ray down. Because it is now forbidden to take over humans, so he claimed, he wanted the descendants to know about the animals. He chose to share the descendants' history. I haven't decided why he did that, but I don't think it was out of kindness. They, the other side, are seeking to close the portals now that all of their original beings have crossed back."

She was greeted with a look of confusion.

"Damn," she said. "I forgot something. It keeps shifting up like debris from the ocean floor." She took a deep breath. "I forgot to explain that when the human body they borrowed died, their energy, which continued, sought a portal. Stories like the Ghost Walker were actually those kids seeing the energy from a hybrid crossing back to its own dimension."

"Here? In Ruthorford?" Dorian asked.

"Yes, apparently, there were a few here. I don't know who." She did, but she wasn't going to admit it.

Eryk, with a gleam in his eye, looked at Sim, "Maybe Sim's not the child of hybrids, but a hybrid himself."

<Bite me> Sim signed.

"I guess we won't really know until he dies," Dorian added to the teasing.

<Yeah, well, remember I'm gonna outlive you, so you'll never know, asshole.> Sim smirked at his friend.

"Children," Teresa said, laughing, and giving them leeway to let off their own angst in the way they did by teasing.

"So, if they are all gone now," John said. "I guess we're officially on our own."

"Why doesn't this make me feel better?" Morgan said.

"And I'm wondering about their rules about choosing their...their...I seem to want to call them victims," Jenn said.

"I don't know much about that. I don't know if it was an energy match or if they observed people. I don't know how they got to them. Could they exist for a time here, like the Gulatega? Again, I'm full of jumbled images, some buried deep." She looked at Sim.

<I'm like you. There doesn't seem to be the chronology we'd expect. Hell, maybe our brains work the same way, storing memories, or maybe it's our brains that have jumbled what he sent. If I figure it out, I'll let you know.> Sim signed to Teresa but open for all to see.

Teresa shrugged. "It is what it is," Teresa answered, repeating what she'd been telling herself over and over.

"I keep going back to it saying that the portals are closed and we're safe. However, that doesn't make me feel better about Meadow going to Scotland to research that cave. Personally, I'm not sure I trust what that entity said," John said.

"If what he showed in the *imagery* was right, that portal should be closed by the time she gets there," Teresa said, trying to reassure him.

"IF is a mighty big word."

Teresa nodded.

"Do we know what happened to Ian?" Morgan asked.

"He didn't make it. Humans can't survive in that dimension. Apparently, they are more energy than we are."

"It's kinda sad. He wanted that so much, from what I understand," Jenn commented.

Dorian spoke up, "Yeah, so much so he kidnapped my wife to get our help. He has no sympathy here."

"What about Ray? Is he okay?" Jenn asked.

"He looked okay. Resolute. He knows we're here if he needs us." Teresa looked at the frown on Jenn's face. "I don't think he will betray our trust, even if he remembers, which I don't think had happened when he left. I don't know how that works. I guess it depends on if the entity wanted him to remember."

"How's Bonnie?" Jenn asked.

Teresa shook her head. "It will take time, but she'll be all right." Teresa knew Bonnie was strong. After all, she was a descendant. She'd survive.

***

The doorbell rang. Frowning, Ray walked over to the door and opened it. Eryk stood in the hallway.

"How in the hell did you get up here?" he asked, thinking of all the security in his building.

"I have my ways," Eryk said, letting the electricity slip from his finger to his thumb. "Want to invite me in?"

No was his first thought, but he knew Eryk would have information he wanted, so he stepped back and held the door open.

Eryk stepped into the penthouse condo, flooded with natural light. Mostly an open concept, Ray's studio took up most of the area. Off to one side was a wall kitchen with a large island with chairs along three sides. A hallway off to the side probably led to bedrooms. "Nice."

"What brings you to Alexandria?" Ray asked, picking up a towel and casually wiping paint from his hands.

"I came up to get Jasmine for Christmas and thought I'd swing by."

"A little out of your way, wouldn't you say?"

Eryk smiled. "Not too bad. How are you?" He said it casually as he walked around, looking at several easels set up around the room.

He nodded to one of them. "I see your vision has righted itself. That's quite a piece." It was a piece similar in style to the Christmas tree one they had in the lobby, with a main item with colors emanating from around it.

"The vision is still different, but I'm adjusting." It was killing him, but he wasn't about to ask.

Eryk moved a little farther into the room. Leaning casually against the floor was a portrait of Bonnie. It was magnificent in its depiction of her softness and empathy.

"Do you even want to know?" Eryk said, turned, and strolled over to the window, looking out across the Potomac. He was fighting his own energy and desire not to wipe the floor with the man casually leaning against the kitchen counter.

"You know damned well I do, but I don't have the right to ask."

It was at that moment that Eryk stepped over to an easel facing the wall. He watched Ray start to move forward and he stopped him with a look. Eryk stepped around the easel.

Ray closed his eyes and leaned back against the counter, gripping the edge so tight he was sure there would be bruises when he let go.

Eryk studied the painting. It was not the abstract that Ray was known for. Other than the one with Bonnie, the studio was filled with abstracts of color. This was of a being, standing in a wavering portal, Ray lying at his feet, while energy from the being fanned out to encompass Ray.

"So, you do remember some." Eryk looked at Ray, studying him for the first time. He'd lost a little weight in the short time he'd been gone. There were dark smudges under his eyes.

"Not much. Bits and pieces are coming back in nightmares and daymares."

"More information than I've got, and I was there," Eryk said simply. "You and Sim hold the keys to that kingdom." He purposefully left out the sisters and Teresa.

Ray snorted. "Not a kingdom I'd think you would want any key to." He looked him in the eye. "I am sorry. For all of your talents, how it came to be must be disturbing." He knew he was reaching out to see if Sim or Teresa had imparted information.

Eryk's shrug held the answer. He returned Ray's look and opted for one of Teresa's statements. "It is what it is."

Ray couldn't stand it any longer. "How is she?"

Eryk saw the pain in Ray's eyes. He slowly shook his head. "More understanding than I would have been. She sees what we did to you as criminal. Oh, she'll forgive us, sooner or later."

"Forgive you?"

"Uh-huh. We used you. I don't know if, from what you have gleaned or remembered, we had much of a choice. I guess we could have tried to use Mike or Jenn to get the creature to go back, but it seemed attracted to you. We've always protected Ruthorford first." In that statement, Eryk let Ray know where he stood. "For that, we're sorry. We had no idea what was going to happen."

Ray let out a laugh, more like a huff. "I don't hold ill will toward any of you. You gave me back my life and then some. The morning I left, I woke up only remembering fighting for control of my being and the need to get as far away from the danger as possible. The feeling grew, and it became a fight-or-flight situation. I chose flight since I didn't know who or what I was fighting."

"I can't say that I blame you. Anyway, I really came by to offer an apology from all of us. Like you, we have to learn to move forward. Things changed for us that day, as well."

"Tell her—"

Eryk held up his hand. "No. I came to offer our apology in person. Anything else is on you."

After Eryk left, Ray took the painting from the easel and moved down the hall. Taking a key, he unlocked and opened a door. He set the canvas against the others that filled the room. Without looking back, he pulled the door shut and, locking it, walked over to the window, staring out across the water, settling the rhythm of his heartbeat, like Bonnie had taught him, as images flooded his mind.

***

It seemed like she'd cried buckets of tears, sitting on her couch, propped on the pillow, the blanket across her legs, staring at the Christmas tree he'd set up for her. How had he just walked away? She'd asked that a thousand times and still had no answer.

A knock sounded on the door. She didn't answer. She heard the door open and the soft click as it closed. Sandra walked into the room. "This package came for you." She set it on Bonnie's lap.

She opened the box. There was an envelope taped to the pretty Christmas paper. She pulled it off and opened it.

<I've never known anyone like you. I never will. Ray>

She set the envelope aside and pulled off the paper. Slowly, a frame appeared. As she pulled more paper away, a portrait emerged—of her—brilliant colors fanning out, like the Christmas picture hanging in the lobby at the B & B. Her dark green eyes stared back at her, seeming to follow her as she shifted the painting. He'd painted her hair sable with gold highlights, her skin dewy, and it looked so soft she wanted to touch it. He painted her lips full with the tiniest upward tilt as if she held a secret no one else knew. The picture blurred behind the tears that filled her eyes.

"My God, Bonnie, he's in love with you," Sandra said, sitting on the coffee table, looking over at the painting.

"He's an artist," she said simply, still staring at the portrait.

"True, he's a very talented artist, but there's more to that painting than art; there's love." With that, Sandra stood, leaned over and kissed Bonnie on the head, and let herself out.

Bonnie stared at the painting. At least she'd known love.

Finally, for the first time in days, she slept.

Bonnie worked Christmas Eve, refusing to sit for the family dinner. Teresa let her, giving her what she needed to heal. She spoke little but smiled politely as she served her friends and family the fabulous feast.

Teresa stepped into the kitchen. "At least come with us to the Christmas Eve service. The kids are singing and you love that. We'll clean up after. It's not going anywhere. Please."

Bonnie nodded. Teresa had already been so gracious, giving her time off. "I'll meet you there."

Slipping into the chapel, she slid into the back row. After hearing the young voices raised in song, Bonnie was glad she'd come. The small chapel was the perfect place to heal. Knowing her sadness, they hadn't asked her to sing this year, the first time in so many years she couldn't count. She looked around her. This was the family she loved, the ones that went out of their way to protect and comfort her.

As they rose to join the singing, she felt movement next to her and heard a familiar voice beginning to harmonize with hers. She didn't turn her head but kept singing. Finally, as they sat back down, she looked over at Ray.

"I just couldn't. I tried. I love you too much." He reached out and joined his hand with hers.

She nodded to the aisle. They slipped out of the chapel, stepping into softly falling snow.

"Are you all right?" She asked, letting herself feel the fast pace of his pulse as they walked down Main Street.

"I will be…someday."

They stopped at Chapters, where he saw his covers still on display.

"I am so sorry."

"Don't. If we hadn't done that, others would have been in danger. I ran. For that, I'm sorry. There's no excuse."

She let out a throaty laugh. "Seriously?" she asked, letting her eyes meet his. This time he looked away first.

Bonnie started walking again. "Now, I'll let you in on a little secret. I coerced Sim—semi-siblings can do that—to share some of his memories with me. I don't know how much he did or if he could even filter it. I wanted to know what you had faced."

He stopped, turning her to him, putting his hands on her arms. "No...." It came out in a breath as he looked at her beautiful face, aglow in the lights from the Elements' tree playing across her face. "No," he whispered and pulled her to him.

She slipped her arms around his waist, letting him hold her for a moment, letting the feel of his arms sink in, something she thought she'd never have again.

She took a slight step back, looking up into his face, the face she loved, taking a chance. "In Ruthorford, there are those called Keepers of Memories. I guess we both fall into that category now. Maybe we can help the descendants understand how they came to be and help them forge a better future. And, together, we can help one another understand those flashes of knowledge we hold."

He thought of all the canvases locked away and remembered the day he and Bonnie created a truer image of the creature than anyone ever had. He took her hand and crossed the street, turning back toward the Bed & Breakfast in front of the old sisters' house, unaware of the flutter of curtains as they passed.

Bonnie and Ray walked back to her apartment, hand in hand, not saying a word. When they stepped inside, he saw the portrait hanging over the small buffet table.

Turning her to him, he said. "Ask me."

"Ask you what?"

"To stay."

"Stay," she said. It came out barely a whisper.

"Forever," he said before he took her mouth with his.

#

To the Happiest of Holidays

And a Future Full of Memories!

Legends

One of the things that makes the small town of Ruthorford special are her legends. I've included three that pertain to this story. Enjoy!

The Legend of the Snowy Owl

by Shanon Grey

Many harvests ago, before the white man came to our land, we seldom ventured in the shimmering hills, where creatures glowed, as does the full moon on still lake water. When the creatures wandered, the people stayed away, for the creatures stole their spirits, leaving the people as children, running naked in the woods, unable to protect themselves from the wolf, the bear, or the coyote. Innocent were these people who forgot their sons and daughters, even their parents. They forgot our ways and our teachings, as a newborn knows only to cry in the night.

One day, a young maiden wandered to the shimmering hills, hunting the herbs to heal. As she climbed the rock mountain, a great white owl swooped from the sky, its giant wings hiding the sun. Its fierce cry frightened the maiden and she ran, dropping her basket of herbs. She ran to the village and told the Chief of this great bird, but he thrust her from him, knowing she had entered the forbidden land and spoke as that of a child. A cry from the sky called to the great Chief and he did look to the clouds and watched them move. The young girl clung to him, pointing to the center of the big white clouds. As they watched, a piece of cloud broke off and fell from the sky. As it came closer, they saw it was not a cloud but a great bird, its wings wide, its yellow eyes piercing. The giant bird circled above them, dipped, dropping something from his feathery talons. The basket of herbs fell at her feet, filled with the healing herbs.

The maiden and the Chief watched the great owl wing its way back into the large cloud and saw that the cloud was not a cloud at all, but many white owls. From that day forth, the white owls flew in great numbers whenever the creatures stirred, warning the people of danger, and allowing the people to roam the hills once more in search of their healing herbs.

And that is how the Snowy Owl became the protector of the people.

The Legend of the Crystal Cave

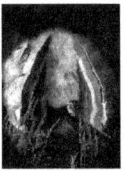

by Shanon Grey

On the other side of the mountain, where the herbs grew wild and plentiful, the mountain's mouth opened in a quiet yawn. No one from the tribe dared cross the granite teeth that framed its mouth, sharp and jagged, threatening to consume those that angered the spirit of the mountain. In return, after a heavy rain, the mountain spewed forth stones that shone in the moonlight and soft golden rocks that sparkled in the sun. The women wove the stones and gold into their clothes, headdresses, and rugs. Life was good.

Then one day, a stranger appeared. The women of the village had gone to the stream to wet the hides and found the man, half-dead, lying in the stream, water slipping over his limp body. They ran to the village and told the chief about the man and gave their leader the small disk they'd found on the ground near the man. It shone like their golden rocks and was etched with an owl on the front. A white owl.

Warriors carried the man to the village, his body burning with fever. His hair, red as the fire that burned in the hut, lay in wet curls about his flushed skin. His eyes blazed green, like many of the stones the mountain spirit gave them.

The man awakened briefly several times, struggling to rise and ranting in a language unknown to the people. He grabbed the Old Mother who tended him, begging something of her, but he would fall unconscious before she could figure out what he wanted. He cried out, over and over, tears running down his cheeks, "Mah bairn lassie."

The powerful medicine man, even with the magic of the mountain herbs, could not keep the man on this plane and he died, burning as if on fire from within.

Warriors, hunting near where they'd found the stranger, heard cries coming from the mountain. Since crossing the stones was taboo, the warriors returned and told the chief and the medicine man, fearing the mountain spirit was angry. The Old Mother, remembering the man's pleas, went to the mouth opening, listening. As only a mother could do, she heard the cries and knew it was not the spirit of the mountain that screamed, but the cries of an infant. With urgings of motherhood overcoming fear, she stepped across the jagged teeth into the black mouth of the mountain.

As she stepped into the narrow opening of the throat, she stopped. Far ahead, a green glow emanated from the bowels of the cave, lighting small stones embedded in the walls. She moved forward towards the sound and the growing light. Just as the passage came to an end, she saw an even narrower opening to the side and stepped through, into a vast cavern. The walls glistened, their light pulsing with each piercing wail. A pool in the center shimmered with dancing lights, flitting across the surface. She hesitated, stunned by the sight, ready to run. But the plaintive cry coming from a stone ledge stopped her. Swallowing her fear, she moved forward, until she stood looking at a child, an Indian child. With trembling fingers, she stroked the tear-stained cheek and the mouth rooted toward her hand and latched on to her old knuckle, making sucking sounds. As the child suckled, her breathing evened and her eyes opened. The Old Mother found herself staring into the same green orbs as the man she'd tended. The room began to darken.

Knowing she wouldn't be able to see to get them out, the Old Mother removed her hand to lift the babe. The child let out a yowl and the room brightened once more. Not letting herself think, the Old Mother grabbed the infant and ran back up the throat, jumped over the teeth, and ran until she reached the safety of the forest. Only then did she stop, her lungs burning.

It was then that she saw the chief and medicine man. She stepped forward, holding the child protectively to her breast. Without a word, they turned and walked back to the village, no one mentioning the child or where she'd come from. The Old Mother silently claimed the infant and cared for her.

As the weeks passed, member after member of her tribe became ill, succumbing to the illness that had taken the life of the stranger. Fear ran through the tribe, many blaming the infant for the fever that claimed the people, from the strongest warrior to the youngest child. The Old Mother did not sleep, afraid someone would sneak in and kill the infant. However, when she heard her own son, a fearless warrior, lay dying, she wrapped the child next to her breast and made her way to her son's hut. His woman fought her entry, but the chief intervened, letting the Old Mother bid her dying son farewell.

As she knelt beside him, he opened his eyes, burning with fever, and asked to see the child she fought so hard to keep. Letting tears fall, she laid the babe on her son's shrunken chest. As soon as the infant touched his body, his eyes grew wide and he gasped a great breath. She grabbed the baby, feeling a thousand stings rush up her arms, tingling her very blood. Her son's woman pushed her and the child out of the hut, cursing the Old Mother.

Her heart heavy, the Old Mother made her way back to her hut, knowing it wouldn't be long before she, too, would burn with fever. She waited, taking joy in caring for the green-eyed infant that made her smile.

She was tending the babe in the sunlight that streamed through the entrance, when a large shadow fell across her, blocking the light. She turned towards the hut entrance. Her son stood in the doorway, as hale as he had been in his youth. He dropped next to her and held her, letting her cry her tears of joy. He gently lifted the babe and helped his mother to her feet. They stepped from the hut to find what was left of her tribe gathered in front of her door. Protectively, she reached for the child. Her son stopped her with a shake of his head as he handed the baby to the medicine man. She watched as the great medicine man took the child and walked through the people, placing her against the chest of each, going first to those too ill to stand.

As he came to the last woman, he stopped, holding out the child. With a nod, the mate of the Old Mother's son took the babe and placed her to her breast, where the child fed noisily. The Old Mother's son brought his mother and joined his mate. He led them home, a family once more. They named the child Tanis, daughter of the mountain.

The sickness left the village that very day. From then on, no other member of the tribe fell ill and those who did or were injured, healed quickly with the simple touch of the mountain child.

Tanis listened as the Old Mother told her stories of the fire-haired man who'd brought her to them, lightly fingering the owl disk she wore around her neck. On the anniversary of her arrival, she would lead the tribe down the throat of the mountain, singing. Her sweet voice made the walls glow and the stones sparkle. She took her place on the ledge, watching her people splash in the pool and, with a wave of her hand, tiny orbs of light would dance over the pool, a promise of happiness and health only she could give.

The Ghost Walker

by Shanon Grey

"Hush!" his voice shushed the girl beside him.

They knelt behind the massive oak in Ruthorford's private cemetery. It was late. It was cold. His hands felt like ice. He glanced down at his best friend and smiled at the rapt attention she'd fixed on the graveyard. Without thinking, he moved his hand and let it rest atop hers, grinning when she jumped.

"Don't do that. You scared the bejeebers out of me," she hissed but didn't move her hand.

Locking hands, they leaned around either side of the tree. "Are you sure about this?" She forced her voice low.

"Yes. Now be quiet," he hissed back. He wasn't sure at all. He'd heard his mom talking on the phone about some ghost walker in the old cemetery and he'd run over to Bethany's as soon as he could get away. It was late and they had school tomorrow. Hopefully, something would happen soon. It was friggin' cold out. His breath hung in front of him with each exhale. Even more hopefully, they wouldn't get caught. It wasn't that this cemetery was off-limits or anything. It was just that this cemetery was for descendants, those in Ruthorford who were directly descended from the founding families. There was another cemetery, a more public one, that sat next to the Chapel. Everyone got a memorial service there. And a headstone. Just that descendants were actually buried out here, in the woods. Never seemed strange to him. It was the way it had always been. He would probably be buried in the public cemetery since he wasn't really a true descendent. Born and raised here, he was as much a part of Ruthorford as anybody. His mom said so. But his dad had been a Navy pilot from Norfolk, Virginia. And his mom was just a distant cousin of a descendant or something. He'd never figured it out exactly. Not like Bethany. She was a descendant for sure, from her tawny skin to her dark red hair. Indian and Scot, all the way.

"I hope they hurry up," Bethany whispered, "I gotta pee."

"Geesh, girl. I thought you went before we left."

"I did. But, it's cold. I need to pee when it's cold."

"Girls," he whispered under his breath.

"I heard that," she whispered softly and squeezed his hand hard, so his bones bunched together.

"Give," he whispered back and she eased up on the pressure.

He looked over at her and felt the first twinges of sadness. This might be their last outing. Things changed when girls went through puberty around here. She looked like she was damned close. Those bumps on her chest were breasts. Not that he objected to breasts. He'd been looking at them for some time now, sneaking peeks at the magazines his brother kept under his mattress. He'd look and get all warm and feel funny inside. Oh, he knew all the right words about what was happening. He just didn't want to think about it. When he thought about it, he thought about Bethany and losing her to some bulked-up descendant.

"Davy." She tugged on his hand. "Look."

In an instant, he scanned the graveyard. "Shit." He wasn't sure if the words had come out or not.

His hand felt clammy and he didn't want to have her holding onto a wet hand, but when he tried to pull away, she clasped a hold on it that wasn't going to break without some pain. He relaxed and let her hold on because, right now, his wet hand was the least of their problems.

On the other side of the graveyard, barely visible, a figure moved. Or a shadow of a figure. He wasn't sure. Although cold, there seemed to be a mist swirling about. He squinted, trying to sharpen his focus. It had to be a ghost. He was kinda seeing through it. It looked cloudlike, kinda lavender.

It moved past a headstone. It had to be a man. It was too tall to be a kid. Its arms hung limp by its sides. Zombie! *Get a hold on yourself, Ackworth. Zombies are fiction. This is no fiction.* He swallowed hard and tried to remember all his science. Nothing came to mind.

As he racked his brain for some logical explanation, the figure walked another ten feet and stopped between two trees. A light shimmered from below. He couldn't tell if it came from the ground or what, a tombstone was in the way.

Bethany fell forward, yanking on his hand. He leaped up to pull her up and stopped dead, holding her in mid-air.

The man had turned and was looking right at them. His eye's glowed purple.

Everything seemed to happen at once. The light underneath the ghost shot up, Davy pulled Bethany to her feet to run, the man disappeared right before their eyes, and a dead silence fell over the graveyard.

Bethany squealed and took off running, pulling him after her. He caught up and ran beside her, adrenalin rushing through his body. Hell, if this was their last adventure, it sure was one hell of a good one.

Shanon Grey

Shanon Grey weaves suspense and action with mystery and romance. Under contract with Crossroads Publishing House and TOVA Publishing House, her books are available in e-format and print at most booksellers.

Shanon spent most of her life on coasts, both the beautiful Atlantic and the balmy Gulf. A major hurricane taught her the fragility of life and the strength of friendship, family, and starting over.

She found out that her son had salvaged notes and pages of her original novel, Capricorn's Child, which she thought had been destroyed along with everything else. (Ironically, a neighbor found her marriage certificate in a tree.) She plans to resurrect her original novel one day.

She now lives in Georgia, trading the familiarity of the coast for the lush beauty and wonder of the mountains, where her husband fulfilled her lifelong dream—to live in a beautiful cottage in the woods, where inspiration abounds.

Having dual careers, one as an author and the other in IT Security, affords her, in her dual personas, to meld expertise from many disciplines and venues into stories that keep her readers coming back for more.

Jerry Hampton, the companion attendant to the alter ego, Shanon Grey, provides the discipline and order to the creativity. She also provides the artistry that does into covers and accompanying materials for web sites, events, and book signings.

Stay up to date on other Shanon Grey books and events by visiting her website at: www.ShanonGrey.com

You can also visit Shanon Grey on Facebook or Twitter @ShanonGrey.

You can write her at shanongreybooks@yahoo.com.

She would love to hear from you.

A Note from Shanon Grey

Thank you so much for reading **Where the Mistletoe Grows.** If you haven't had the chance, I hope you will feel compelled to enjoy my other stories. I started my journey in Ruthorford, with her descendants, which continues to grow and evolve. I have many stories yet to tell, and not just about Ruthorford, as you can see. My writing has enabled me to make incredible friendships with my readers, as well as others I've met along the way. I can't begin to tell you what that means to me. Your feedback is always encouraged and welcomed. I love hearing from my friends. Write me at shanongreybooks@yahoo.com.

Please help others learn about my stories. If you've enjoyed them, I encourage you to take a moment to leave a review at your online retailer, such as Amazon, as well as Goodreads. Every review helps. Also, we can never underestimate the value of word-of-mouth. Tell others. I love having as many friends as possible.

Shanon Grey

SHANON GREY

THE SHOPPE OF SPELLS ~ available in digital and print

Morgan Briscoe's relatively normal life is turned on its ear when she learns not only was she adopted, but her birth parents are dead and she now holds half-interest in a business with their ward, *Dorian Drake*, who, despite his riveting good looks, can barely conceal his hostility toward his new partner.

Morgan discovers that she is more than she seems and together she and Dorian have the ability to control a portal to another dimension. Unable to control their growing attraction, Morgan and Dorian dance around their desires and her burgeoning abilities, until danger forces them to face their destiny.

MEADOW'S KEEP ~ available in digital and print

Jasmine Monroe once felt like damaged goods. Not anymore. Her latent abilities, although appearing too late to save her from a brutal attack, now keep her safe from anyone hurting her again. Secure in that fact, she's moved on. Until she meets her first love's doppelganger.

Eryk Vreeland, a misfit and an embarrassment to his upper-class/upper-crust family, is a magician. His shows are renowned, his contributions to charity astronomical, his illusions precise. Except—his is real magic. Forced together to rescue a young woman, safeguards must come down and, when that happens, their attraction strengthens—beyond their control—until they can barely tell where one person stops and the other begins. Will they surrender to a legacy or risk a disaster to stay apart?

PENNYROYAL CHRISTMAS ~ available in digital

A Ruthorford Holiday Story

Kateri Chance comes back to Ruthorford for a fresh start and runs into the man that caused her to leave in the first place. She must resolve her past before she can move forward. However, someone doesn't want that to happen. Join Kat as she explores Ruthorford, the small town that protects its own.

GLYNDA'S DARE ~ available in digital and print

Everything gone, *Glynda* heads north, hoping that fate might be kinder this time around. A knew job and a new life outside of a small southern town, Glynda discovers that southern charm does extend as far as Georgia, as do good-looking men. When *Tom* rescues Glynda from the hooves of an angry stallion, Glynda begins to believe that her shattered heart might have a chance to heal after all. But her past is coming back to haunt her and could likely get her killed.

Fortunately, the she has landed in the arms of people who protect their own, whether they want it or not and Glynda finds she's got help on her side, if she's just willing to take a chance.

TWISTED FATE ~ available in digital and print

Ruthorford – the perfect southern town, with even more perfect descendants. Except, perfection has come with a price. Now, in order to survive, they must turn to outsiders for help.

A missing body and an accident that looks like a set-up force the powers that be to call in someone who can do it all – with the help of the descendants. Things never appear quite as they seem and, at every turn, things start heating up – in the investigation and between those that should know better. Welcome to Ruthorford – where science and magic merge.

258